THE MAGIC OF LOVE

'I love you until there is nothing in the world but you!'

When Melita Cranleigh arrived in Martinique to begin a new life as a governess, she was apprehensive of the future and afraid of what her new employer would be like.
Étienne, Comte de Vesonne, proved to be young and distinguished. Her nightmare quicky turned into an exciting dream as they were drawn like a magnet towards each other, heart, mind and spirit as one.
But as the drums beat out their primitive message, Melita found her happiness threatened by the jealousy of Madame Boisset, cousin to the man she adored, and the rituals of Voodoo which cast their dark shadow over slaves and plantation alike...

The Magic of Love

by
Barbara Cartland

MAGNA PRINT BOOKS
Long Preston, North Yorkshire,
England.

British Library Cataloguing in Publication Data.

Cartland, Barbara   1902—
    The magic of love.
    I. Title
    823'.912 (F)

    ISBN 1-85057-353-0
    ISBN 1-85057-354-9 pbk

First Published in Great Britain by Pan Books Ltd. 1977.

Copyright © 1977 by Cartland Promotions.

Published in Large Print 1989 by arrangement with the copyright holder.

Printed and bound in Great Britain by
Redwood Burn Limited, Trowbridge, Wiltshire.

Author's Note

I visited Martinique in 1976 and found it to be the beautiful, mysterious and haunting island of flowers I have described in the book.

My son and I stayed at Leyritz which I have described under the name of Vesonne-des-Arbres. Previously a plantation, the eighteenth-century house has been restored and made into an hotel in the last five years by clever and attractive Madame Yveline de Lucy de Fossarieu.

The slave quarters are chalets and the store house is a very attractive dining-room. It has been described as a Shangri-la, and it is not surprising that when President Giscard d'Estaing of France wished to entertain President Ford of the U.S.A on French soil he took him to Martinique and lunched at Leyritz.

When I arrived I found in the beautiful Salon of the main house an exhibition of dolls made of leaves like those I have described in this book.

They were made by the Assistant Manager, a young coloured man, and they ranged from a replica of Queen Elizabeth I to one of

Josephine Baker.

St. Pierre, the Paris of the West Indies, was destroyed by the eruption of Mont Pelée in 1902 when 30,000 people were killed in three minutes. Some of it has been re-built, but its gaiety and importance has been transferred to Fort de France.

To me Martinique is one of the most fascinating places in the world.

CHAPTER ONE

1842

As the ship slowly moved into the harbour Melita stood on deck and looked with delight at the island ahead of her.

She had expected Martinique to be beautiful but it exceeded all her expectations and was in fact the most beautiful place she had ever seen.

The town of St. Pierre had been built in a crescent shape between a curving beach and a correspondingly curving hill which was verdant green against the vivid blue of the sky.

Towering to the left of it was Mont Pelée, which meant, as Melita had learnt, 'Bald Mountain', from a bare spot near its summit.

An unromantic name, but the rest of it was vividly green with trees which included those she was longing to see like the mahoganies, gum-trees and the 'fromagers', besides banana, mango and coconut trees.

All the way from England the officers on board ship had regaled her with stories of the beauty of Martinique and its strange, mysterious rain forests.

Now she was entranced with the town of St.
Pierre, and while she was standing looking at
its white houses with their red roofs and the
high twin turrets of what she thought must be
the Cathedral, a ship's officer said at her side:

'It's called "The Paris of the West Indies".'

'It is very beautiful!'

'It's also very gay,' he laughed and went on
his way.

It had been a strange and at times very
frightening voyage, and yet Melita thought
she would never forget the kindness that had
been shown to her by the ship's officers and
the other passengers on board also.

At first she had been too unhappy at the
thought of leaving England and too frightened
of what the future held to seek companionship.

She had stayed in her cabin feeling helpless
and numbed by the swift tide of events.

Then with the elasticity of youth she had
known that somehow she had to face what lay
ahead and it was no use trying to avoid it.

So she had gone up on deck to feel the bitter
December winds in her face and find that their
very roughness gave her a new courage.

She had experienced a different kind of fear
when they met a storm in the Atlantic which
had threatened to capsize the ship.

10

It had been so terrifying that Melita, like most of the passengers, had felt that their last hour had come.

And yet by sheer good seamanship they had survived, and when they moved into tropical waters the sunshine, the emerald and blue of the sea and the brilliance of the sky had swept away the memory of their terror.

But now Melita knew she was afraid again, afraid of what she would find in Martinique, afraid most of all of her unknown employers.

The very word sent a little shiver down her spine.

What would it be like to be employed? To have to do someone else's bidding, to be ordered about knowing that one dare not answer back or refuse to obey.

For a moment it seemed as if the sunshine that enveloped the town ahead was dimmed and she wished that she could run away from what was waiting for her.

But where could she run?

She knew there was nowhere.

She could hardly believe it was possible that her life could have changed so dramatically from the first week in December.

It was then that her Stepmother had told her what she had in her mind.

'I want to talk to you, Melita,' she said, and

11

Melita had known instinctively from the hard note in her voice that what she was about to say was unpleasant.

She had known as soon as her father married again that her life was not going to be easy, and that between her and this strange woman who was attempting to fill her mother's place there was already an antipathy.

She had known it as the new Lady Cranleigh came flouncing into the house in Eaton Place and had seemed so large and overbearing when Melita compared her to her small, gentle, sweet-faced mother.

'So this is Melita!'

There was something disparaging in her tone, something which told Melita all too clearly that her Stepmother was not impressed by her appearance.

'My dearest,' her father had said, 'you received my letter?'

'Yes, thank you, Papa. You told me you were to be married. I of course wish you every possible happiness.'

'I am sure we will be very happy,' her father said a little awkwardly.

Melita knew that he was embarrassed and had no wish to talk of his marriage.

Responsive as she always was to her father's moods, she said:

12

'There are sandwiches and drinks waiting for you in the Study, Papa. I thought you would not wish for anything very substantial as dinner will be ready in an hour-and-a-half.'

'I shall need a bath and someone to unpack for me,' the new Lady Cranleigh answered almost aggressively, as if she suspected she was being neglected.

'A housemaid is waiting upstairs,' Melita explained, 'and the footmen are carrying the trunks up at this moment.'

'Perhaps I had better see to it.'

'There is really no need,' Melita answered, but even as she spoke she realised she had said the wrong thing.

Her Stepmother had no intention of allowing her, a mere child of seventeen, to arrange anything for her and she made that abundantly clear in the days that followed.

When Melita was alone with her father she longed to ask him why he had married again, and why he had chosen this bossy, self-assertive woman who was in complete contrast to everything her mother had been.

But there was no need to ask the question.

She learnt all too quickly that her Stepmother had money, and what was more, she was related to a number of very important families, including that of the Foreign Secretary.

13

Melita had always known that her father was ambitious, but now she realised how far his ambition could carry him, although she was quite certain that in the first instance he had been the pursued rather than the pursuer.

'I shall just have to make the best of it,' she told herself with a sigh.

None of them, neither Melita, her father nor Lady Cranleigh, had envisaged how little time there was to be to make the best or even the worst of the situation in which they found themselves.

A year after he had married for the second time and a year ago this Christmas Sir Edward had died.

It had been such a shock that even after Melita had followed her father's coffin to the grave-side she could hardly believe it was true.

Always when she came back to the house she expected to hear his voice, and at night she would sometimes go to his bed-room to make quite certain she had not been dreaming and that he was in fact there and alive.

Now in deep mourning only a year after she was a bride the new Lady Cranleigh, as she said herself, 'faced the tragedy with fortitude'.

She certainly had a large number of friends to console her and the fact that she looked extremely attractive in black was no doubt some

14

compensation for the loss of her husband.

To Melita it was as if the light had gone out of her life.

She had thought when she lost her mother that nothing would ever be the same again, but when her father went it was as if the mainstay and prop of her very existence had been swept away from beside her with one blow.

She and her father had always been very close, and wherever he was appointed in his diplomatic career Melita went with him, and however busy he was he always had found time for her.

It was an agony after he died to look back on how happy they had been in Vienna and what trouble he had taken to explain to her in Italy the history of its great monuments and buildings.

He had made the past come alive because he was not only a very distinguished Diplomat but also a notable scholar.

After he was dead Melita's only consolation was to read the books in his Study and try to imagine that he was explaining them to her as he had done during his life-time.

It was perhaps, she thought later, because she found so much consolation and interest in reading that her Stepmother had decided her future.

She had felt too unhappy and miserable to join the tea-parties which even while she was in mourning Lady Cranleigh continued to give every Thursday.

She was in fact seldom asked to join the small but amusing dinner-parties which even a widow could give without outraging the proprieties.

Then, one December morning, when the sky was grey and even the big fires in every room at Eaton Place could not keep out the chill winds, Lady Cranleigh dropped what was to Melita a bomb-shell.

'I have been thinking of your future, Melita,' she began and her eyes as she rested them on her stepdaughter's face held an undoubted expression of hostility.

This was due, Melita had realised without being conceited, to the fact that in the last two years she had grown very pretty.

Her fair hair which resembled her mother's was like spring sunshine and her eyes, which were a very dark blue, seemed to fill her small face with its delicate pink-and-white skin which reminded people of Dresden china.

She was exquisitely made and walked with a grace which might have been envied by a ballerina.

'Thank God you move like a dancer,' her father had said once. 'I cannot bear clumsy

16

women who rise from a chair as if they are activated by wires.'

Melita had laughed, but she knew what he meant.

Her mother had seemed to float into a room as if she was a piece of thistledown and she always hoped that she emulated her.

She was in fact a complete contrast to her Stepmother who was heavily built and was likely in middle-age to grow heavier still.

'My future?' Melita questioned.

'That is what I said,' Lady Cranleigh replied. 'I do not know if you have any ideas on the subject.'

'I do not...think I...understand.'

She had imagined, because there was no alternative, that she would live with her Stepmother and make her début this Season, which she had been unable to do last year because she was in mourning.

It had always been planned that she would be presented to the Queen at Buckingham Palace, after which she would attend the innumerable Balls and Assemblies that supplied the background to other débutantes in the Social World.

'I think we had best be completely frank with each other,' Lady Cranleigh said, 'and I will start by telling you that I have no intention at

17

my age of being a Dowager or a Chaperon to a young girl.'

Melita looked at her wide-eyed.

'I do not...think there is...anyone else who would bring me out,' she said after a moment. 'Papa always said he had very few...relations alive and Mama's family, as you know, came from Northumberland.'

'I think you would find it difficult to inveigle anyone, even if you had a relative willing to do it, into introducing you to Society when there is no money to pay for it,' Lady Cranleigh said.

'No...money?' Melita questioned.

'I have been closely into your father's affairs,' Lady Cranleigh replied, 'and I find that when everything has been settled and the mortgage on this house paid off there will be nothing left for you.'

Melita clasped her hands together.

She had known after her mother's death, when she was coping with the finances of Eaton Place, that it was in fact too expensive for them, but her father had not listened.

When she made suggestions for moving into a smaller house he ignored her, and so they drifted on hoping that something would turn up and that one day they would be solvent.

Now Melita saw only too clearly that her father had been living in a fool's Paradise.

18

There had never been any chance of his making enough money to clear up the debts that had steadily accumulated, unless of course he should marry a wealthy wife.

That in fact was what he proceeded to do and there was no doubt that in the year of his second marriage he had been more opulent than at any other time in his life.

Looking back Melita realised how many more luxuries they had then compared with the previous years.

Her father had not only given her delightful and exquisite presents, he had also spent a considerable amount of money on her clothes and the horses he gave her to ride.

Now uncomfortably Melita realised, as she had not understood before, that everything she received had been paid for not with her father's money but with her Stepmother's.

Lady Cranleigh was watching the expression on her face.

'I see you understand,' she said, 'and while during your father's life-time I was quite prepared to pay for his daughter, I do not intend to continue to do so now that he is dead.'

Her face hardened as she continued:

'What is more, I will tell you quite frankly that I do not want you living here in this house with me.'

'Then...what am I to...do?' Melita asked helplessly.

'That is what I intend to tell you,' Lady Cranleigh answered, 'and quite frankly, Melita, you have no alternative but to agree to my suggestion.'

Melita waited apprehensively.

She had the feeling, although she could not be sure of it, that Lady Cranleigh was embarrassed by what she had to say.

Nevertheless she was determined to say it.

'When your father and I were in Paris three months before his death,' Lady Cranleigh said, 'we met there a charming man, the *Comte de* Vesonne. He told me that he had a small daughter to whom he was apparently devoted.

'He talked about her to your father and they both agreed that the most important part of a girl's education was to acquire an ability to speak languages.

'When we parted he said to me: "When Rose-Marie is a little older, *Madame*, I shall beg you to find an English Governess for her. I would wish her to speak English as well as French, and when she grows older there are other languages I shall add to her curriculum." '

Lady Cranleigh paused to say:

'I think you are beginning to guess what

20

plans I have made for you.'

Melita was incapable of answering her Stepmother, who went on:

'Last August I wrote to the *Comte de* Vesonne and told him I had found what I thought would prove to be an excellent Governess for his daughter. I received an answer two days ago. He has asked me to despatch the Governess as soon as possible to St. Pierre in Martinique!'

'Martinique?'

It was difficult for Melita to say the word.

'You mean...I should go there alone to live with people I have never...seen?'

'For Heaven's sake, girl, you have to grow up sometime!' Lady Cranleigh replied.

'B.but it is...too far away,' Melita managed to say.

Lady Cranleigh shrugged her shoulders.

'That, as it happens, suits my purpose. I have no wish for people to say that I have driven you into earning your own living, and there are certain to be those who because they are jealous of me will suggest that I ought to chaperon you and find you a suitable husband. But I am too young for that, Melita—far too young!'

She was, Melita knew, at least thirty-five, but she had the feeling these past months that her

21

Stepmother was determined to marry again and she could understand only too well that she did not wish the encumbrance or indeed the competition of a younger woman.

Melita had risen to her feet to walk across the Breakfast-Room.

'Surely there is...something else I can...do?'

'You could go into a Convent, if you would prefer to incarcerate yourself in a kind of tomb. I certainly will not stop you.'

'No...no, I could not do that,' Melita said, 'but Martinique...it is the other side of the world.'

She saw the expression on her Stepmother's face and knew that was what had recommended it to her as a decidedly suitable situation.

'I have...never taught anybody. What do I know about teaching?'

'The child is not very old,' Lady Cranleigh retorted, 'and I should have thought with all that reading you do and the trouble and expense your father took over your education you would know enough to be able to impart it to some little Creole who is not likely to be very intelligent.'

'But supposing the *Comte* and *Comtesse* do not like me?' Melita said. 'What shall I do then?'

'You had better make sure they do, unless

you are prepared to swim home,' Lady Cranleigh said.

She too rose to her feet and looked at Melita with undisguised hostility.

'I have already replied to the *Comte's* letter to say that you will be on the ship that leaves Southampton in two week's time. I will pay your passage to Martinique and I will give you £100. That is more than is left in your father's estate and you may think yourself very lucky to have it!'

'And when that is...spent?' Melita asked.

She turned to face her Stepmother almost piteously as she asked the question.

At that moment a pale gleam of winter sunshine came through the window to illuminate her fair hair almost as if it was a halo.

She looked very lovely and very insubstantial.

'You can starve in the gutter for all I care!' Lady Cranleigh said in answer to her question and went from the room slamming the door behind her.

It had seemed to Melita in the days that followed that she moved in a nightmare from which she could not awake.

As she supervised the packing of her trunks, taking with her not only her own treasured possessions but also everything she could that

23

had belonged personally to her mother, she thought it could not be happening.

She could not be leaving England perhaps for the rest of her life, and she had visions of being so inadequate a Governess that she was dismissed and of seeing the £100 melting away before she found other employment.

'I shall starve,' she thought frantically.

Then she remembered almost as a comforting thought that there was always the sea.

It would not be too hard to die if she could join her mother and father. At least she would not be alone as she was alone at the moment in a hostile world where there was no-one to whom she could turn for help.

Vaguely she thought of trying to get in touch with her cousins and any other relatives she must have in Northumberland. But then she remembered that to them she would be merely an encumbrance, an unattached woman without money, and she shrank from contacting them.

But there was in fact no time for her to do anything except obey her Stepmother's instructions, pack her boxes and travel to Southampton.

Because she suddenly felt extremely ignorant and quite incapable of teaching anyone, even a young child, she packed a number of her father's books feeling by doing so even in the new world she would not lose contact with him.

They made her feel more alone and more unhappy than ever as she touched the well-thumbed pages. Those which had been their favourites brought the tears to her eyes.

She could hear his deep voice reciting lines of poetry to her which he knew, because they were so close, she would enjoy as much as he did.

'Oh, Papa, Papa,' she wept, but she knew that there was nothing she could do except carry out her Stepmother's plans.

Up to the last moment she had had a feeling that perhaps a miracle would save her, but when the ship finally sailed out of Southampton harbour she had been too blinded by tears to take a last glimpse of the land of her birth.

There had actually not been much to see because it was a grey, drizzly day, the sky was overcast and the sea as dark as steel.

By contrast the great rollers breaking on the beach at Martinique were the colour of Melita's eyes and the sky was a translucent blue that was unlike any colour she had ever seen before.

As the ship slowly nosed its way towards the long jetties she saw the innumerable little boats in the harbour, some of them with their sails up running before the wind, others moored to buoys, and a large number of three-masted schooners anchored near the shore.

There were pennants and flags fluttering from their mastheads and they gave the harbour an air of festivity, which made it seem almost as if St. Pierre was *en fête*.

'The Paris of the West Indies,' Melita said to herself, then she knew that whatever the town was like it would not concern her.

She had learnt by studying the letter which the *Comte* had written to Lady Cranleigh that the house or *Château* where she was going was not in St. Pierre, but some way outside.

'I myself, will meet the lady you are sending us,' (the *Comte* had written in an elegant, educated hand) *'and I assure you, Madame, we will do everything in our power to make her feel at home.'*

'At home!' Melita thought scornfully. How could she ever feel at home amongst strangers in a strange land?

And yet even if Martinique was strange it was certainly beautiful.

Although she had been frantically busy with her packing before she left London, she had found time to go to Moody's Library in Mount Street to ask if they had any books on Martinique.

The Librarian, who had often helped her before in finding books that she and her father wanted to read, searched and searched, but could find nothing that was particularly helpful.

There were just a few paragraphs in an encyclopaedia and a map which, he admitted himself, was not likely to be very accurate.

Nevertheless the map had seemed to Melita to give her a better idea of the island than she had had before.

She found St. Pierre marked quite clearly, and a little to the north of it there was Mont Pelée. To the south there was another town and harbour marked 'Fort de France'.

The history of the island, told briefly and badly, was that Martinique had been discovered by Christopher Columbus in 1502. Finding the natives, who were called Caribs, unfriendly, he did not stay there.

It was not until later that Martinique was colonised by the French, and afterwards it had been captured several times and taken over by other foreigners including the English.

But finally it had returned to France and remained French territory.

Melita had visited Paris with her father, but he had never had a diplomatic post in France, and she wished now that she knew more about the French.

They had seemed charming, delightful, courteous people, but she had not been grown up when they had visited Paris, and she had met no-one socially but Diplomats.

What did she know of the ordinary people? She had a feeling that they were different in every way from the English. After all, their countries had been enemies and from time to time at war for many years.

'Suppose they dislike me just because I am English?' Melita said to herself apprehensively.

She knew she was nervous in a way she had never been nervous in her life before, as the ship drew nearer and nearer to the Jetty.

She went down below to her cabin and put on a cloak of silk taffeta which had been made in the latest fashion before she left London.

She was determined that, whatever else, she would not appear in her new position looking like a crushed, miserable Governess who was utterly dependent on the whims of her employers.

So she had sold a small diamond ring which had belonged to her mother, and spent the proceeds on clothes.

When her Stepmother realised what she had done she sniffed and said scathingly:

'If you like to dissipate your only assets on personal adornment, I shall not stop you! But do not ask me for more money, for I have no intention of giving it to you!'

Melita had not replied, but she had thought to herself that she would rather die than go begging to her Stepmother.

For the last year while she had been in mourning all her clothes were black, and those she had worn previously were either too young for her now or quite unsuitable to be worn by a Governess.

She realised that the climate of Martinique would be hot and she therefore bought yards of voiles and muslins to make into gowns during the long voyage.

Although her father had taught her from books, her mother was an expert needle-woman and had taught Melita to sew.

'Every woman should be able to use her needle,' she had said once, 'and, dearest, you will find it useful in life to be able to make your own gowns should you ever have to do so.'

Her mother had just been talking vaguely, Melita had thought at the time. But now she wondered if perhaps she had been clairvoyant enough to know that one day her daughter would be very glad of such a feminine accomplishment.

The silk taffeta cape had been expensive and her bonnet with its decoration of soft lace which framed her face not only looked expensive but was also extremely becoming.

There were blue ribbons tied under her chin and when she went up on deck carrying a leather bag which contained her money and her jewels she knew that while her heart was thumping apprehensively and she felt very young and very afraid, she looked a Lady of Fashion.

The Jetty and the Quay beyond were crowded with people and Melita went to the rail of the ship to look for her future employer.

She had asked her Stepmother to give her a description of the *Comte*, but she had been vague, perhaps purposely so, Melita thought.

'Quite a nice-looking man, about your father's height,' she had answered coldly. 'I cannot tell you anything more about him. All Frenchmen look alike to me!'

'Has he any other children besides the one I have to teach?'

'I really have no idea,' Lady Cranleigh replied. 'I was not particularly concerned with the *Comte* at the time. It was only after your father's death that I thought he might be useful—as indeed he has proved to be.'

'I do not know if he is young or middle-aged,' Melita thought.

She told herself, however, re-assuringly, that

he would undoubtedly find her and when the gang-plank was put down great crowds of people swarmed up it and onto the ship.

There were not only those meeting the passengers; there were porters, ships' clerks, salesmen and a number who, Melita thought, had just come aboard out of curiosity.

The ship's crew tried to prevent the influx, then gave up the unequal struggle.

A steward brought Melita's luggage from her cabin and set it down beside her.

'I think that's everything, Miss.'

'Yes, it is,' Melita replied, 'and thank you very much for looking after me so well.'

She gave him two guineas which she felt was the least she could do after a long voyage, and he thanked her profusely.

'I hope, Miss, you'll enjoy your holiday,' he said as he pocketed the guineas.

'Holiday!' Melita thought bitterly. 'It is a life-sentence!'

She stood waiting a little apart from the gang-plank, but now there was no longer a crowd coming aboard and those who had found the people they had come to meet were beginning to leave the ship for the Quay.

Melita looked with anxious eyes at a large fat Frenchman with a very loud voice who was conversing with a sailor.

31

He had an absurd little pointed moustache and looked like a blown up balloon, and she hoped fervently that he was not her future employer.

But he was there for nothing more important than to collect a huge parcel, and a few minutes later he carried it down the gang-plank, sweating profusely as he did so.

The air was hot and moist, but not unpleasantly so.

There was a cool breeze from the sea and Melita could see the palm-trees moving gracefully. Beside them were a number of other trees in blossom which she thought very beautiful.

But it was difficult to be concerned with what was happening ashore when she was waiting anxiously to be collected and there was no sign of her future employer.

'Supposing there has been a mistake,' she thought fearfully, 'and he has not come to meet me? Or supposing after all they have changed their minds and do not want me?'

She felt so apprehensive that she looked around praying that she would not be left un-collected for much longer. Then she saw a tall man with a top-hat at a rakish angle talking to one of the ship's officers.

She had not noticed him come aboard. Now she thought in fact he was the most distinguished of any of the men she had seen coming up the gang-plank.

His long tube-like trousers were in the very latest fashion and his embroidered double-breasted waist-coat was not unlike one she had often seen her father wear.

But she could only see him in profile, and now he turned at something the ship's officer said and looked towards her.

'This cannot possibly be the man I am expecting!' Melita thought wildly. 'He is far too young and far too attractive!'

But astonishingly he was walking towards her and she realised she had not been mistaken in thinking he was one of the most attractive men she had ever seen.

With dark hair and dark eyes, his face sunburnt against his white collar, he was the personification of elegance as he moved across the deck.

Only as he reached her side did she realise that, if she was staring at him in surprise, he was looking at her in complete and utter astonishment.

'Pardon me, *Mademoiselle*,' he said, sweeping his hat from his head, 'but I am told that your name is Miss Cranleigh.'

'That is right,' Melita said, 'and you...?'

'I am *Le Comte de* Vesonne!'

Melita curtsied, but the *Comte* was still staring at her.

'You are really the Miss Cranleigh whom I am expecting—the lady who has come to Martinique as Governess to my daughter?'

'I am Melita Cranleigh, *Monsieur*, and my Stepmother wrote to you about me.'

'*Nom de Dieu!*'

The exclamation seemed to be jerked from his lips. Then he said in a different tone:

'Forgive me, but I cannot credit that you should be so young. I was expecting someone of middle-age.'

'My Stepmother...Lady Cranleigh...did not tell you...?'

'She told me that she could provide me with a very suitable Governess for my little girl, one who was intelligent, experienced and whom she could thoroughly recommend! But she did not say that you were your father's daughter.'

Melita's lips tightened.

She knew only too well what had happened.

In her desire to rid herself of her stepdaughter Lady Cranleigh had deliberately omitted to say who she was and that she had in fact not yet passed her nineteenth birthday.

'I am...sorry that you should be...disappointed,' Melita said uncomfortably.

The *Comte's* eyes looked down into hers and

they were twinkling.

'I am not at all disappointed,' he answered, 'I am astonished and perhaps I should add—delighted! Come, let me take you ashore. We can talk it over later.'

'Yes...of course,' Melita agreed.

She looked vaguely at her luggage lying beside her, but the *Comte* snapped his fingers and a porter appeared from nowhere.

The *Comte* reached out and took a leather case that Melita carried in her hand, then preceding him she walked towards the gang-plank.

When she reached it she saw there one of the ship's officers who had been very kind to her on the voyage.

'Good-bye, Mr Jarvis,' she said. 'I would like to thank you for a very pleasant voyage, and will you please convey my compliments to the Captain?'

'I will indeed, Miss Cranleigh, and I wish you every happiness on this beautiful island.'

'Thank you,' Melita replied.

She went down the gang-plank and when she reached the Jetty she turned to look at the *Comte* who was just behind her.

'You have more luggage than this?' he asked.

'A great deal more...I am afraid,' Melita answered.

'A porter will find it,' he said.

He gave instructions to the man and they waited on the Quay while Melita's trunks—five large ones—were brought from the hold of the ship onto the Jetty.

'I hope it will not be too much for your carriage?' she asked nervously.

'I have brought a carriage with me which will carry it without any difficulty,' the *Comte* answered, 'and I suggest that as it is now twelve o'clock we should send the carriage on to Vesonne and you and I will have something to eat here before I take you there in my chaise—that is if you do not mind an open carriage?'

'I would love it!' Melita answered. 'I would like to see the country-side. It looks very beautiful!'

The *Comte's* eyes were on her face and there was an expression in them which made her feel a little shy.

She had a feeling, although it was quite absurd, that he wanted to say that she was beautiful too. Then she told herself she was just being conceited and he was still astonished that she was so young.

The carriage was strongly built and drawn by two horses. There were two servants in attendance and there was plenty of room for Melita's boxes on the top and at the back and for her hand-luggage to go inside on the cushioned seats.

The *Comte* saw it safely stored away, then he took Melita to where his chaise was waiting.

It was very smart and dashing and not unlike the chaises she had seen the young men of Paris driving in the Bois.

The *Comte* handed Melita in and took the reins, and the groom who had been holding the horses jumped up onto the seat behind.

Melita noted that he wore a livery with crested buttons and a cockaded hat not unlike those worn by their own servants at home.

They drove along the streets and now Melita had a glimpse of the large building with two turrets she had seen from the ship; she had not been mistaken in thinking it was the Cathedral. The Town Hall also was very impressive with a large clock over the front door.

The homes all had red tiled roofs and the windows were without glass as was usual in tropical climates. Many of the streets were narrow and crooked, but the one along the water front was wide and shaded with trees brilliant with blossom.

Everywhere there were flowers, the vivid red of hibiscus and the purple, pink and orange of bougainvillaea.

'So! What do you think of it?' the *Comte*

asked as they had driven a little way in silence.

'It is...lovely...far more lovely than I expected,' Melita said.

'You come from London?'

'Yes.'

'And you really think it compares favourably with such an awe-inspiring City?'

'I was comparing it with Paris,' Melita answered. 'I am told it is called the "Paris of the West Indies".'

'It is a good imitation—but nevertheless an imitation!' the *Comte* said.

'You would prefer to be in Paris?' Melita asked.

'At times,' he answered with a smile, 'but at others I am quite content with the sunshine and the gaiety of Martinique.'

'You have lived here for a long time?'

Melita felt that she was asking a lot of questions but she was very curious.

'My father came to live in Martinique before I was born,' the *Comte* answered. 'But I often visit Paris—in fact I was educated there.'

Melita was about to ask him some more questions when she realised that it was hardly her place to show curiosity and that he should be asking her about herself.

But before they could say any more he drew up outside a Restaurant on the sea-front.

It looked typically French on the outside with coloured sun-blinds. When they entered it was to find the tables were set out in a court-yard in the centre of which there was a small fountain and whose sides were banked with flowers.

'How pretty!' Melita exclaimed involuntarily.

'I promise you that the food is as good as it looks,' the *Comte* said with a smile.

The Proprietor hurried forward.

'*Bonjour, Monsieur le Comte!* Your usual table is ready for you,' he said. '*Bonjour, Madame!*'

'My guest *Mademoiselle* Cranleigh has just arrived from England,' the *Comte* said, 'and this is the first place she has visited. I would not like her to be disappointed.'

'*Mais non, Monsieur le Comte!* It is impossible that she should be. *M'mselle* shall have the best *repas* that she has ever enjoyed.'

They were led to a table in an alcove.

The walls were bright with murals skilfully executed and the bougainvillaea trailing everywhere made it a bower of colour.

'When I left England it was grey and cold, and the fogs in November had been very bad,' Melita said in a wistful tone.

The *Comte* smiled at her.

He had set his tall hat down on an empty chair and put Melita's bag beside it.

It had been her mother's and was very opulent-looking, made of crocodile skin, and had her initials on it.

'What have you brought with you in this?' he asked. 'The Crown Jewels?'

'No, only my own, *Monsieur,*' Melita replied, 'and they are very small and almost non-existent.'

'They are certainly contained in a very impressive case.'

'It was my mother's.'

'Was she beautiful—like you?'

Melita blushed.

'You make it...impossible for me to...answer that question.'

'You must tell me all about yourself,' the *Comte* said. 'I am still astonished at your appearance. Was I really very stupid in imagining you would be very different? Or was your Stepmother deliberately evasive as to your appearance and your age?'

Melita was surprised that he should be so perceptive.

'My Stepmother...wished to get...rid of me,'' she said in a low voice.

'I can understand that,' the *Comte* replied.

Again she thought how strange it was that he should be able to grasp the situation so quickly without explanations.

'So she sent you to the other side of the world,' he said. 'I always thought that Martinique was especially favoured by the gods!'

'Are there gods in Martinique?' Melita asked, anxious to change the subject because she felt embarrassed. 'I thought there would be only Voodoo which came with the slaves from Africa.'

'We have that too,' the *Comte* answered. 'Plenty of it, as it happens, but I like to think that the gods who dwelt on Olympus also dwell on our high mountains. They have conical peaks and when the clouds are low they look mysterious and exciting.'

'I shall look forward to seeing them,' Melita said.

'I will show them to you,' he answered.

She looked across the table and found that her eyes were held by his.

She had the feeling that once again the world in which she was moving was unreal; only this time it was not a nightmare but a dream—a very exciting dream from which for the moment she had no wish to awaken!

CHAPTER TWO

Like all Frenchmen, the *Comte* concentrated on choosing the meal with the greatest care.

'First,' he said to Melita, 'you must taste our Matoutou of crab.'

'I like crab,' she answered.

'In Martinique we eat land-crabs,' he said. 'They are kept for fifteen days in a barrel where they are fed with mangoes, pimento and corn. I think you will find them delicious.'

He then went on to choose chicken with coconut served with Ratatouille Creole, which was a profusion of vegetables and herbs fried in oil and garlic. Melita found the dishes unusual, but as delicious as the food she had eaten in France with her father.

'Now,' the *Comte* said, 'as you are new to Martinique you must eat bananas.'

'I have often eaten bananas,' Melita replied.

'Have you?' he questioned. 'There are many sorts of bananas here: green served with salt, pepper and chutney; yellow, very ripe and simmered in wine to which is added cinnamon; uncle-bananas or *bananes-cornes*, which are bananas shaped like horns.'

Melita laughed.

'Please stop...I agree I have never eaten bananas!'

They drank wine with the meal, but first of all the *Comte* insisted on Melita having a drink made with fruit juice and rum which she thought was cool and delightful.

'Rum makes people happy,' the *Comte* said, 'which is why you will find the Martinicans are always smiling.'

Melita had noticed as she came from the ship and as they drove along in the *Comte's* chaise that everyone she looked at appeared to be showing a large expanse of gleaming white teeth.

'Does rum really make people feel happy?' she asked seriously.

'Rum combined with sunshine and peace in one's home,' he answered.

There was something in the way he said the last two words which made Melita feel they were said with intent, and because she felt a little guilty that she had not asked before she said quickly:

'Will you tell me about your daughter?'

'Her name is Rose-Marie,' the *Comte* said. 'She is eight years old and I find her adorable and very attractive.'

She would certainly be that, Melita thought, if she was anything like her father.

She had never imagined that she would be having luncheon alone with a man who was not only so exceedingly handsome but whose eyes seemed to change continually with everything he said.

They were dark in colour, and yet when something amused him they seemed to twinkle with lights which came from the sun itself.

'Is Rose-Marie an only child?' Melita enquired.

'I have no other children, unfortunately,' the *Comte* answered. 'When you see Vesonne-des-Arbres you will realise that the place was made for a large family and I adored it when I was a boy.'

'You had brothers and sisters?' Melita asked.

'My brother unfortunately died when he was seventeen,' the *Comte* replied, 'but I have four sisters, all of whom are now married and living in Europe.'

'You must miss them,' Melita said sympathetically.

'I do.'

There was silence for a moment. Then Melita said a little nervously:

'Will your...wife...*Madame la Comtesse*... think me too young to look after Rose-Marie?'

44

She knew that ever since she saw the *Comte's* astonishment at her appearance there had been a definite fear at the back of her mind that he and his wife might find her unsuitable and send her back to England.

'My wife—died three years ago.'

Melita was still.

This, she realised, was something else her Stepmother must have known but had not told her.

Perhaps she looked apprehensive, for the *Comte* said quickly:

'Her cousin, *Madame* Boisset, who is a widow, runs my house—and the estate.'

There was a little pause before the last three words and now there was a definite shadow in the dark eyes and Melita felt in some way that the laughter had left his lips.

'I am...sorry about your...wife,' she said nervously, 'and will *Madame* Boisset explain to me what I am to teach Rose-Marie?'

'I will do that,' the *Comte* said positively. 'I have very definite ideas on the subject. I wish Rose-Marie to be brought up in the way that I have planned for her and I will not stand interference from anyone else!'

He spoke sharply, but as he saw the apprehension in Melita's wide eyes he said more quietly:

45

'I am sorry. I do not wish to make you nervous, *Mademoiselle*. Suppose we start at the beginning and you tell me about yourself?'

Melita dropped her eyes shyly.

'There is really very little to tell,' she said. 'My father, as I think you know, re-married and when he died last year he had spent all his money. There was nothing left for me.'

'But your Stepmother is rich?'

Melita glanced at the *Comte* for a moment, then looked away again.

'She is...young...she did not wish to...chaperon a Stepdaughter.'

'I can understand that, but is it really necessary for you to earn your living?'

'Very necessary,' Melita replied.

'It seems strange,' the *Comte* said reflectively, 'when I remember how important your father was in diplomatic circles and how warmly other Diplomats spoke of him, that you should be obliged to seek employment as a Governess.'

'I...I could think of nothing else...that I could do,' Melita said frankly.

'You did not think of getting married?' the *Comte* asked.

There was a little pause before Melita answered:

'I have been in deep mourning this past year

46

and have been nowhere, so I have not met any gentlemen who might have...offered for me.'

There was a little silence between them. Then the *Comte*, as if he was at a loss for words, signalled to the waiter to fill up their glasses with wine.

'No more, please,' Melita said putting up her hand.

'You are sure?' the *Comte* asked.

'I am not certain if it is correct for a Governess to drink at all,' she answered.

'You are on French soil,' the *Comte* replied, 'and, as you know, everyone in France from the lowest and poorest peasant has his bottle of *vin* every day.'

'That is what Papa told me,' Melita said, 'but it is strange to think that Martinique is French and retains French customs when you are so far away from France.'

'Only if you measure it by miles,' the *Comte* replied. 'Our hearts belong to our own country.'

Melita smiled at him.

'Perhaps it is the exiles who love their own land best,' he added, 'and that is why we must do everything in our power to prevent you from feeling homesick.'

'I shall try not to be,' Melita said seriously. 'At the same time it is a little...frightening not knowing what to...do or how to...behave.'

'I think you will find that all you have to be is yourself,' the *Comte* answered, and the way he spoke it was a compliment.

She thought she should change the conversation from herself.

'What do you grow on your estate. *Monsieur?*' she asked. 'The ship's officers told me on the voyage that the main crops on the island were sugar, bananas, coffee and spices.'

'They were quite correct,' the *Comte* approved. 'Actually on my plantation we mostly grow sugar cane, bananas and a little coffee.'

'It sounds very interesting,' Melita said, 'and can you manage to find labourers? I understood that Martinique does not have a very large population.'

'At Vesonne-des-Arbres there are plenty of slaves.'

'Slaves?' Melita exclaimed. 'I thought...' She stopped.

'What did you think?' he asked.

'I thought that the slaves on these islands had all been freed.'

'They have been in Antigua and some of the other islands,' the *Comte* replied, 'but not yet in Martinique.'

'But, surely...' Melita began.

Then she realised it would be rude to discuss

slavery with a slave owner.

She knew that her father had had very strong views on the subject, and she had believed that practically all over the world it had been accepted that slavery was cruel and an offence against human dignity and that all slaves had been set free.

As if once again the *Comte* knew what she was thinking he said:

'Slavery will ultimately be abolished in Martinique as it has been in other places, but at the moment it is being fiercely debated by the Government and until they make a decision, individual owners are powerless to do anything about it.'

'I...understand,' Melita said in a low voice.

'I hope you do,' he answered, 'and when you see the slaves at Vesonne you will realise that they are in the main a happy community—at least I think so.'

He spoke in a manner as if he was not directly concerned with them and Melita was puzzled.

She thought perhaps there was some mystery about Vesonne, then told herself she was just being imaginative.

They finished their meal and Melita said:

'Thank you for one of the most delicious luncheons I have ever eaten; it was exciting

49

because it was so new.'

'There are many new things I would like to show you...' the *Comte* began.

Then he stopped abruptly and Melita thought perhaps he had suddenly remembered that it would be a mistake for him to be on such intimate terms with his child's Governess.

'I must not forget I am only a superior sort of servant,' she thought, and tried to recall how her own Governesses had behaved.

In retrospect they seemed to her rather dull, unassuming women, who realised almost as soon as they arrived that they knew less about some subjects than their pupil.

While they had taught her to the best of their ability, Melita had relied on her father for everything that appertained to Literature, the Classics, especially Poetry, and Mythology.

Languages she learnt automatically in the countries in which they were posted, as her father always insisted upon her being taught by teachers in their mother-tongue.

But where French was concerned he had chosen teachers for her in London and in Vienna, and it was a sense of relief for Melita to know that in that language if in none other she was in fact bilingual.

The *Comte* was looking at her and it seemed as if he read her thoughts since he said:

'Shall I compliment you on your French accent, which is truly Parisian? Although it is after all what I might have expected from your father's daughter.'

'Thank you,' Melita said, 'but I shall never be able to emulate Papa fully, who spoke seven languages perfectly and knew a great many of the Southern-European dialects.'

'You must start Rose-Marie on English,' the *Comte* said, 'and I am afraid she is not very proficient at any of the essential subjects like Arithmetic, Geography and Music.'

'You consider music to be an essential subject?' Melita asked.

'For a woman? Yes.'

'Why more than for a man?'

She was talking as she would have talked to her father, intently and perhaps provocatively, for they had loved to argue with each other.

'I think that music is part of a woman's whole composition,' the *Comte* said. 'She should talk rhythmically and move rhythmically. Music can harmonise not only her whole body but also her mind and character.'

'I think you are right, although I never considered it from that angle before,' Melita said reflectively.

'And yet you move as if you were compelled to do so by a melody singing in your heart.'

51

His voice was deep and low as he spoke.

Melita looked at him, her eyes widened, and somehow it was hard for her to look away.

She had never imagined a man's eyes could be so dark and yet so expressive, and at the same time irresistibly compelling.

Very slowly the colour rose in her cheeks. Then there was the sound of laughter from an adjacent table and the spell was broken.

'Perhaps we should be moving,' the *Comte* said, 'it is fifteen miles to Vesonne-des-Arbres and even with my fast horses it will take us over two hours.'

They left the Restaurant and once they had started driving along the waterfront Melita found it very hot.

The waves were rolling in onto the beach and there was a majesty about them which Melita found very impressive.

Then they turned inland and now very short-ly she was shaded from the sun by the trees growing on either side of the road.

The horses were climbing and the road was passing through strange, exotic vegetation.

Now at last Melita saw what she had been seeking: corossol, guava and mango trees, bread fruit and avocados. Then these were suc-ceeded by what appeared to her to be a jungle.

Now there were bamboo, filso and flamboyants, royal palms and tamarinds. White giant ferns grew to enormous heights forming at times almost a tunnel over their heads.

When they went downhill into deep gorges there would be a silver stream sparkling over rough rocks.

Never had Melita imagined that vegetation could be so extraordinary or so profuse and the *Comte* pointed out the 'fromagers' which he told her could reach 30 metres in height, and the arborescent ferns which were often 10 metres long.

He also showed Melita the parasite plants, vines and other epiphytes which entwined themselves round other plants and shrubs, eventually strangling them.

'The law of the jungle!' the *Comte* said. 'Even plants, like humans, live on each other and only the strongest survive.'

He spoke almost harshly and Melita said softly:

'It is all so beautiful. I cannot bear to think that where there is such beauty there must also be cruelty.'

'Nature is cruel—human beings are cruel,' the *Comte* replied. 'They suffer and inflict suffering.'

There was a pain in his voice that was unmistakable, and as they ascended from a deep gorge Melita glanced at him from under her eye-lashes.

'He seemed at first to be gay and carefree,' she thought, 'a lighthearted man.'

But now she was not sure.

There was something which convinced her without obvious evidence that he was suffering.

But why?

'Perhaps I shall never know,' she told herself with a sigh. 'After all, it is not for a Governess to be curious about her employer's emotions or feelings.'

'You are very quiet,' the *Comte* said a little later. 'What are you thinking?'

'I was thinking how strange this is,' Melita replied. 'At the same time I am naturally a little ...nervous about what lies ahead.'

'You do not feel like an adventurer exploring a new territory, thrilled at the idea of discovering what you have never known before?'

'I try to feel like that,' Melita answered honestly, 'but I am so afraid of failing...of making mistakes.'

'I will help you not to make any,' the *Comte* said as if he spoke impulsively.

Then he added:

'If I am there.'

'You mean you do not live at your plantation? Is that the right word for it?' Melita asked.

'It is the right word, and I am there—part of the time.'

'But, surely there is a great deal for you to supervise?'

Coming over in the ship she had heard stories of how hard the Planters worked and how difficult it was to get the crops to market at the right time and in the right condition.

'I thought I already told you,' the *Comte* answered, 'that my wife's cousin runs the estate.'

'A woman?' Melita exclaimed in surprise.

'Yes, a woman! She is in charge!'

Now there was no mistaking from the tone of the *Comte's* voice that the idea did not meet with his approval.

'There is something strange here,' Melita thought to herself.

But she was too shy to question him further and after a minute or so, as if with an effort, he pointed out to her the vivid red of the anthurium flower.

It looked not unlike an arum lily in shape but was vividly scarlet with a white stamen.

They drove on, moving inland and then for the first time Melita saw crops, great bunches of bananas hung from the trees and huge sugar canes with graceful, sword-shaped leaves moved softly in the wind.

Everywhere there were patches of colour, bougainvillaea climbing over walls and up the trunks of trees, large hedges of hibiscus vividly red or golden yellow, and occasionally an orange lily which the *Comte* told her was called '*Sceptre aux Fleurs*'.

As if he wished to entertain her the *Comte* told her amusing stories of Creole life and how Louis XVI had granted Martinique the right to establish a Colonial Assembly.

'We are very proud of our island,' the *Comte* said, 'and if one is happy in oneself, I believe it could be a Paradise for most men and women.'

Before she could prevent herself, Melita said:

'You are not happy?'

He turned his head to look at her as if he wondered why she had asked the question, and she realised with a quick sense of relief that he did not think it impertinent.

'No—I am not happy,' he answered, 'and doubtless you will find out why after you have been at Vesonne for a short time.'

She looked at him with a worried expression on her face and he said gently:

'Will you promise me something?'

'Yes, of course,' Melita answered.

'It would be wise to ask me what I wish you to promise before you give me your word.'

'Then shall I say I promise...if it is...possible for me to do so?'

'That is better!' he said with a twist of his lips.

'What do you want me to promise?' Melita asked.

'That you will not be frightened or too perturbed by what you find at Vesonne. I want you to stay. I want you to realise that although things may be difficult I will always help you if I can.'

He spoke very seriously and after a moment Melita said in a low voice:

'Why should it be...difficult?'

'You will find that out when you arrive,' he answered. 'But I want you not to leave, although you may wish to do so.'

'I want to stay,' Melita said, 'and I have...nowhere else to...go.'

She felt that the *Comte* did not find this answer particularly consoling in whatever was worrying him.

He drove for some minutes without replying, his eyes on his horses moving ahead. Then he said:

'It may seem extraordinary that I should say this, but I know that coming here has been a momentous step for you and I think perhaps it will prove to be a momentous step for me as well.'

'I do not...understand,' Melita said.

'I have a feeling,' the *Comte* said slowly as if he was thinking out the words for himself, 'that you will make me fight for what I know is right, and not just accept what is wrong because it is easier to do so.'

Melita longed to ask him what was wrong and what was right, to explain what he was saying to her.

But she was very sensitive to other people's feelings and she knew instinctively that he did not want to answer such questions now.

And yet in some strange, obscure manner he seemed to be trying to prepare her for what lay ahead, to fortify her against the difficulties—whatever they might be.

Now they were leaving the forest with its strange vegetation behind and moving through more cultivated land, although every now and then the road plunged down into a gorge.

There once again there were the ferns, the tamarinds and the hot, humid atmosphere which smelt entirely different from the land which was cultivated.

They had in fact been travelling for two-and-a-half hours when they turned off the road up a rough, sandy track that had been washed by torrential rains until it was rutted and uneven.

The chaise swung from side to side precariously, until they passed over a bridge to find a plantation of bananas on one side of the road and a profusion of green coffee trees on the other.

Melita looked at the *Comte,* and after a moment he said:

'You are now on the Vesonne-des-Arbres estate!'

They drove for about a quarter-of-a-mile until ahead of them Melita saw a number of buildings.

The first was long, low and built of grey stone and she had the idea it was a store-house.

Bougainvillaea and vines were growing up the walls, and a moment later she saw that beside it there was a huge water-wheel turning slowly, the silver water dropping iridescent in the sunshine into a narrow gully beneath it.

There were more large buildings and then on the left a number of smaller ones with wooden roofs.

She glanced at them with interest and the *Comte* explained:

'The slave quarters!'

Now Melita could see a number of small black children playing on the grass. Then on an incline surrounded by trees in bloom and overlooking all the other buildings she had her first glimpse of what she knew was the main house.

It was two storeys high, built of red brick, with a tiled roof and a verandah, and surrounded by a garden which was a riot of colour.

They passed through an archway, and with a flourish the *Comte* drew his horses to a standstill beside the verandah.

'Welcome to Vesonne-des-Arbres!' he said quietly.

Melita wanted to tell him how attractive she thought it was, but before she could speak there was a cry from the doorway and a woman came running across the verandah.

'Étienne!' she exclaimed. 'I was not expecting you!'

She was, Melita decided, perhaps thirty-seven or thirty-eight years of age, and although she moved quickly she had a thick figure and her face was not particularly attractive.

Her eyes were dark and shrewd and her hair, although dressed fashionably with ringlets on either side of her face, was lank against a sallow skin.

The *Comte* handed his reins to the groom before he replied:

'I have brought *Mademoiselle* Cranleigh

60

back with me.'

'I imagined that was what you were doing,' *Madame* Boisset said in a very different tone of voice, 'when the carriage arrived without her.'

For the first time Melita realised that she had been expected to travel back to the house in the carriage and although the *Comte* had met her at the ship he had not actually intended to drive her to the plantation.

Now *Madame* Boisset looked at Melita for the first time as she stepped out of the chaise and curtsied.

'*You* are Miss Cranleigh?' *Madame* Boisset asked, and there was an accusing note in her voice.

'Yes *Madame*.'

'That is impossible? You are far too young to be a Governess. This is ridiculous!'

The expression on her face reminded Melita of the way her Stepmother looked at her.

She was not quite certain what words she should use to apologise for her youth and perhaps also for her looks.

'I thought you said Lady Cranleigh was sending a woman of a sensible age,' *Madame* Boisset said to the *Comte*.

'I think, my dear Josephine, we would be wiser to discuss this matter, if it needs discuss-

61

ing, inside the house,' the *Comte* suggested.

'It must certainly be discussed,' *Madame* Boisset said sharply.

Nevertheless she led the way inside the building and Melita looked about her in surprise.

The room they had entered was large and obviously a Salon, for it had damask-covered sofas and chairs and a number of pictures on the walls.

There was no glass in the windows, and their covering consisted of large wooden shutters which Melita was sure were only necessary in the event of a storm.

The walls were papered and there were many attractive ornaments, Sèvres china, bibliothèques of French origin standing on tables of the Louis XIV period.

It was very attractive and Melita wished to look about her with delight, but it was impossible not to be aware of *Madame* Boisset's anger.

Now she was saying to the *Comte* in a voice that rose high and shrill with her indignation:

'This is quite absurd as you well know, Étienne! How can this girl possibly be a proper Governess of the sort we were expecting from England?'

'I have talked with *Mademoiselle* Cranleigh,' the *Comte* replied coldly, 'and I find her extremely intelligent. I think she would prove a capable and competent teacher for a child much older than Rose-Marie.'

Madame Boisset made a sound that seemed to combine frustration and irritation in equal parts. Then she said rudely:

'I cannot understand why Lady Cranleigh should have sent us anyone so young. She must be deranged!'

'Lady Cranleigh is the Stepmother of *Mademoiselle*,' the *Comte* said before Melita could speak, 'and as she is Sir Edward Cranleigh's daughter, I am sure in her case that age has little to do with ability.'

Madame Boisset looked Melita up and down and there was no doubt of the hostility in her expression.

'Now I understand, Étienne, why we are honoured with your presence so unexpectedly,' she said unpleasantly.

The *Comte* ignored her and said to Melita:

'I would like you to come upstairs and meet my daughter.'

With a nervous little glance at *Madame* Boisset, Melita followed him from the room and out into a hall where there was a carved wood staircase curving up to the floor above.

There was no carpet on the stairs and it seemed to Melita as if their footsteps sounded unnaturally loud as they went up, leaving *Madame* Boisset staring after them.

Only as they reached the landing did Melita say in a low voice:

'It was wrong of my Stepmother not to explain who I was and my age. You would at least have had the chance to tell me not to come.'

'Shall I say I am delighted that you have?' the *Comte* asked, 'and I know Rose-Marie will be pleased too.'

They went along the passage, at the far end of which he opened a door.

It was a large room and seemed to Melita to be filled with expensive toys of all sorts and descriptions.

There were dolls and teddy-bears, there were balls and bricks and skipping-ropes, a most elaborate doll's-house and of course a rocking-horse.

Sitting at a table having a meal with a black woman was a small girl.

When she saw who stood in the doorway she gave a scream of sheer delight.

'Papa! Papa!'

She jumped up from her chair and ran towards him holding out her arms.

He bent down to pick her up so that she could kiss him almost frantically as if she had been half-afraid she would not see him again.

'You have come back!' she said between her kisses. 'You have come back, Papa!'

'Yes, I have come back,' the *Comte* replied, 'and I have brought someone specially for you, someone I know you will like very much.'

Rose-Marie looked at Melita with her arms still round her father's neck. She was a pretty child, with dark brown hair, and brown eyes.

'Who is this?' she asked after a moment.

'It is *Mademoiselle* Cranleigh—and she is going to give you some lessons, Rose-Marie, and teach you many things you need to know.'

'Is she the Governess Cousin Josephine told me about?'

'Yes, the Governess,' the *Comte* agreed.

'But Cousin Josephine said she would be old and very strict, and would make me do all the things I do not want to do.'

'I think you will find that *Mademoiselle* will show you how to do lots of new and interesting things which you have never thought of before,' the *Comte* said.

Melita smiled at Rose-Marie who stared at her solemnly.

The *Comte* looked over her head at the black woman with whom she had been having tea and who had now risen from the table.

'How are you, Eugénie?' he asked.

'Well, Master, I thank you.'

65

'That is good!' the *Comte* said, 'I shall want you, Eugénie, to help *Mademoiselle* Cranleigh and tell her where everything is.'

'I help *M'mselle*,' Eugénie said with a glance at Melita.

'Thank you very much,' Melita said. 'It is very kind of you.'

She held out her hand as she spoke and after a moment of surprise Eugénie took it and dropped a curtsey at the same time.

'What a lovely School-Room,' Melita exclaimed. 'I have never seen so many toys.'

'Have you brought me a present, Papa?' Rose-Marie enquired.

'Not today,' the *Comte* replied, 'at least I have, only her name is *Mademoiselle* Cranleigh!'

Rose-Marie laughed.

'That is a funny present,' she said, 'and a very big one.'

'You will find your new present is very engaging,' the *Comte* said, '*Mademoiselle* can play the piano, and I am quite certain, although I have not asked her, that she can dance.'

'I like to dance,' Rose-Marie said, 'but I do not like to practise my scales. They are dull— very dull!'

Melita saw at the far end of the School-Room there was a piano and she went towards it, noting that it was a good make.

'I hated scales too when I was your age,' she said, 'but perhaps I can teach you to learn them another way.'

Rose-Marie scrambled down from her father's arms.

'What do you mean—another way?' she asked.

'In a tune.'

'Show me! Show me!' Rose-Marie commanded.

Melita flashed an apologetic little glance at the *Comte*, then sat down on the piano-stool.

She had taken off her gloves and now she ran her fingers over the ivory keys and remembered the little song she had learnt years ago which incorporated the scale as a child went upstairs and another scale when he came down.

She played it but said the words as she was too shy to sing them. Nevertheless it captured Rose-Marie's imagination and after a moment she said:

'I like that! I like it very much!'

'Then that is what I shall teach for the next time you play to your father and you can learn the words to sing them to him at the same time.'

'That is fun—really fun! Play it again, *Mademoiselle*, please play it again!'

Melita was just about to oblige when the door of the School-Room opened and *Madame* Boisset came in.

'I cannot imagine what is happening,' she said, 'there is much too much noise, and it is time for Rose-Marie to be getting ready for bed.'

She spoke in a loud voice and then said pointedly to Melita:

'I hope, *Mademoiselle*, you are not going to start by breaking the good habits I have already instilled into Rose-Marie. Health is the first consideration where a child is concerned.'

Melita had risen from the piano-stool and now she stood feeling a little uncomfortable at what she knew was a direct personal attack.

'I am sorry, *Madame*,' she said. 'I am afraid I had no idea of the time.'

She wanted to say that it was far too early for any child of eight to be going to bed, but she thought that would be needlessly provocative.

Madame Boisset looked at the table and said:

'Finish your supper, Rose-Marie, and I imagine, *Mademoiselle*, that you will wish to retire to your room and see to your unpacking. When you have finished, if it is not too late, I will give you instructions regarding Rose-Marie. Otherwise, they can wait until

68

tomorrow morning.'

'I shall do that,' the *Comte* said in a quiet voice.

'You?' *Madame* Boisset ejaculated. 'Why? Why should you wish to interfere?'

'Because Rose-Marie happens to be my daughter,' the *Comte* said, 'and I have, as you know, very definite ideas on how she should be educated.'

'But if I am to bring her up...'

'You have been doing so while there has been no-one else,' the *Comte* interrupted. 'But now I have engaged *Mademoiselle* Cranleigh and I intend to discuss Rose-Marie's future education with her.'

'You have engaged *Mademoiselle?*' *Madame* Boisset said pointedly and it was a question.

'As you know, I answered Lady Cranleigh's letter and it was my idea to have an English Governess.'

'And I suppose you intend to pay her!'

'Yes, I will pay her myself,' the *Comte* said.

Madame Boisset laughed and it was an ugly sound.

'With your gaming wins, I suppose,' she sneered, 'and what happens when you lose?'

There was something so unpleasant, Melita thought, in the two people sparring with each other that she was not surprised to realise that

Rose-Marie who was standing beside her was trembling.

This was something which had often happened before, she thought, and impulsively she bent down towards the child to whisper in her ear:

'When I have unpacked I have some things with me in my luggage which I know will please you.'

She saw Rose-Marie's eyes shine with excitement.

'Things from across the sea?' she asked.

Melita nodded.

'From Paris?'

'No, guess again.'

'I know—London!'

'That is right,' Melita smiled.

She tried to concentrate on Rose-Marie but she could not help hearing *Madame* Boisset say scornfully to the *Comte:*

'I thought you had left us. Your remarks on leaving were that you did not intend to come back.'

'I have changed my mind,' the *Comte* said. 'This is my home and this is where I belong.'

There was a moment's silence. Then *Madame* Boisset said in a very different tone of voice:

'That is what I told you before, but you would not listen to me.'

70

Deliberately, it seemed to Melita, the *Comte* looked away so that he would not see the expression in *Madame's* eyes. Then he said to Rose-Marie:

'Come, I am going to take you for a walk in the garden. I want you to show me the flowers by the fountain. They were in bud when we looked at them three days ago, but now they should be in bloom.'

'I will show you! I will show you!' Rose-Marie cried excitedly.

She took him by the hand and drew him towards the door.

'It is time for Rose-Marie to go to bed,' *Madame* Boisset said, but there was not such a positive note in her voice as there had been before.

'We will not be very long, Josephine,' the *Comte* said coldly.

Then father and daughter had gone from the room and Melita could hear Rose-Marie chattering as they moved together down the passage.

'What that child needs is discipline,' *Madame* Boisset said firmly, 'and I suppose, Eugénie, you have been spoiling her as usual.'

She looked at the table as if trying to find fault and said:

'I have told the Chef to send her up a plain

71

supper. This is much too elaborate for a child of her age.'

'*La petite M'mselle* will not eat what she does not like, *Madame.*'

'Then she should be made to do so,' *Madame* Boisset said firmly, 'and I hope, *Mademoiselle*, you will see to it.'

She gave Melita a look as if she thought it was very unlikely she would see to anything, and walked out of the room without another word.

Melita looked at the black servant and found that Eugénie was smiling.

'You come with me, *M'mselle*, and I show you your bed-room. I help you unpack, but I expect Jeanne has started already. The trunks arrived over an hour ago.'

Eugénie was right in her assumption.

When she showed Melita the room next door they found that the bed-room seemed to be filled with trunks and there were two maids lifting out Melita's gowns and personal possessions.

'You bring lot of things with you,' Eugénie remarked.

'I was coming a long way,' Melita replied, 'and I could not leave my treasures behind me.'

'We look after you, *M'mselle*, and make you happy in Martinique,' Eugénie said.

There was something sincere in the statement which made Melita smile.

'I hope you will help me, Eugénie,' she replied, 'I shall enjoy looking after Rose-Marie, but I shall need your assistance and you must tell me what time she gets up and when she has her meals. I have my own ideas but I do not wish to annoy *Madame* more than necessary.'

'*Madame!*'

There was a wealth of expression in the one word, and Eugénie made a gesture with her hands which told as surely as if she had spoken that it was impossible to please *Madame* whatever one did.

'Why should she be so disagreeable?' Melita wondered to herself. 'And why should she and the *Comte* fight in such an undignified manner? And in front of the servants, too!'

She knew that her mother would not have approved of such behaviour and she had seen already that it was extremely bad for Rose-Marie.

She was quite certain that her post was not going to be an easy one, and she wished she did not feel so inexperienced and so inadequate.

At the same time it was a comfort to know that the *Comte* would support her as he had said he would.

She took off her bonnet and cloak and was relieved to find that the pretty voile gown she had made herself was not creased despite the long journey.

After she had tidied her hair she said to Eugénie:

'What do you think I ought to do now?'

'I think, *M'mselle*, you should go and join *Monsieur le Comte* and *la petite M'mselle* in the garden. When he is tired of playing with her he will wish to hand her over to you. Then you and I will put her to bed.'

'Thank you, Eugénie,' Melita replied.

She went down the stairs where she found a door in the hall which led into the garden.

She could hear Rose-Marie's laughter and the *Comte's* deep voice long before she saw them.

Finally she found that at the end of a green lawn, half-hidden by great bushes of flowering shrubs beyond there was a most breathtaking view.

She looked over the plantation to where perhaps a mile-and-a-half away there was the vivid blue of the sea, and beyond it an indefinable horizon.

She stood for a moment feeling it was impossible to go any further until the beauty of it was impressed on her memory.

Then Rose-Marie appeared round the side

74

of the bushes and flowering shrubs and saw her.

'*Mademoiselle!*' she cried. 'Come and see what Papa and I have found.'

She took Melita by the hand and dragged her round a bush to where on the side of a small stream was sitting a very large green frog.

The *Comte* looked up as Melita appeared and she saw his eyes rest on her bare head. She was glad she had tidied her hair and that it fell on each side of her face into natural ringlets.

Because she had so much hair and it was so long, Melita arranged the rest in a bun at the back of her head.

Somehow it made her neck seem longer and more delicate and gave her a grace and a poise that was not so obvious when she wore a bonnet.

The *Comte* was looking at her and she would not have been a woman if she had not realised that there was a glint of admiration in his eyes.

'It is a frog, *Mademoiselle!*' Rose-Marie exclaimed. 'A very big frog! Papa says it might turn into a fairy Prince!'

'I think perhaps he is happier being a frog,' Melita answered, 'and I expect he has a lot of baby frogs hidden somewhere, if we could find them.'

'Oh, let us find them!' Rose-Marie said excitedly, running a little way down the stream

75

and peering under the stones.

'What do you think of my daughter?' the *Comte* asked Melita.

'She is very sweet!'

'That is what I find, but I will not have her taught the wrong things or made to behave unnaturally.'

Melita looked at him.

'What do you mean by that?' she asked.

The *Comte* hesitated for a moment. Then he said:

'My wife was a quiet, gentle person. Everyone in the house and on the estate wished to please her. They would do anything she asked of them. There was no need for anyone to be bullied into carrying out her wishes.'

He did not have to say who behaved in the way he disliked, Melita thought.

'I want Rose-Marie to be like her mother.'

'I will do my best,' Melita said. Then because she could not help it she added: 'But it may not be...easy.'

'I know that,' he answered, 'but I am relying on you. Shall I say it more plainly? I have every confidence in you and I will support you in every way I can.'

'Thank you,' Melita said, 'but I do not want to cause any...trouble.'

'There will always be trouble here at Vesonne-des-Arbres while certain conditions exist,' the *Comte* answered. 'But I want you to try to forget them and do what you think is right for Rose-Marie.'

'I will try,' Melita promised.

They were simple words, and yet she almost felt as though they were as solemn as if she had made him a vow.

She looked up at him, at his dark hair silhouetted against the blue of the sky, and once again her eyes were held by his.

Something indefinable passed between them, something which made Melita feel as if her heart was beating unaccountably quickly.

It was hard to break away, and yet she managed it.

She moved across the green grass to find Rose-Marie searching amongst the stones.

'There are no little frogs—none at all!' she said dismally.

'We will come and look for them tomorrow,' Melita promised. 'Now I think we should return to the house. Eugénie is waiting for us.'

'Will Papa come too?' Rose-Marie enquired.

Melita looked back.

The *Comte* was standing where she had left him. His eyes were on her face and there was an expression in them that she dared not translate to herself.

77

CHAPTER THREE

The sun was pouring in through the window of the School-Room as Melita gave Rose-Marie her breakfast.

There was a big bowl on the table containing many fruits she had not tasted before, including pawpaw.

She had discovered with joy when she woke up this morning that from her bed-room window she had the same breathtaking view that she had seen from the garden the previous evening.

The sea and the sky were azure blue and the green of the plantation was so vivid that she felt it could hardly be real.

When they had finished breakfast Rose-Marie said apprehensively:

'Cousin Josephine said that we were going to do serious lessons this morning. Does that mean they will be very difficult?'

Melita had the idea that *Madame* Boisset was deliberately putting Rose-Marie against her.

She realised that because it had been the *Comte's* idea that his daughter should have an

English Governess, *Madame* had obviously been against it from the very outset.

It had not improved matters when Melita had arrived in the *Comte's* chaise looking so young and attractive, rather than the stern martinet with whom she had tried to frighten Rose-Marie.

Now she smiled at the child beguilingly and said:

'I have an idea. As this is my first morning here you shall give *me* a lesson.'

'How can I do that?' Rose-Marie asked.

'Well, I think the first thing you must do is to show me round Vesonne-des-Arbres, explaining to me what all the buildings are for and helping me to explore the garden.'

'I would like to do that,' Rose-Marie said giving a little skip of excitement, 'but will that really, truly be a lesson?'

'I think we could make it one,' Melita said, 'if I told you what some of the things were called in English and you tried to remember them. For instance, do you know what Vesonne-des-Arbres means in English?'

'Yes, I know that,' Rose-Marie said quickly. 'Papa told me. It means "Vesonne of the Trees".'

'That is very good!' Melita said. 'Now if you try to remember one or two more English

79

words, you can tell Papa when you next see him how clever you have been.'

Rose-Marie was obviously captivated with this idea and they set off in the sunshine hand in hand.

There had been no sign of *Madame* Boisset this morning for which Melita was thankful. She hoped that she would not see them escaping from the house and probably send them back to the School-Room.

Rose-Marie wore a straw hat on her head tied under her chin with pink ribbons, but Melita fancied she would look too smart in any of her bonnets.

She therefore carried a sunshade to protect her from the sun which she was sensible enough to realise was too strong for her fair skin.

Rose-Marie took her first to the Chapel.

Built of grey stone, it looked somewhat austere outside, but the chancel was decorated with murals done, Melita thought, many years ago, and the altar with its six high candles was carved in wood and painted.

There were flickering lights in front of the statues of Saints and the fragrance of incense.

'Do you have a Service here every Sunday?' she asked.

'The Priest comes from Basse Point to say Mass on Sundays,' Rose-Marie replied, 'but

Cousin Josephine makes the slaves say prayers outside on the mound with her every evening at five o'clock.'

'Every evening?' Melita asked in a surprised tone.

Rose-Marie nodded.

'She says they have wicked black souls and need prayers more than other people.'

Melita thought this was a typical sort of attitude she would expect *Madame* Boisset to adopt, but she was too wise to criticise her to Rose-Marie, and only said gently:

'I do not think God minds what colour people are. He loves us all.'

'He does not always love me,' Rose-Marie replied, 'not when I am naughty.'

'He does love you,' Melita insisted, 'but He is just disappointed and a little sad when you are not as good as you should be.'

Rose-Marie slipped her hand into Melita's.

'Shall I tell you a secret,' she asked. 'You will not tell Cousin Josephine?'

'No, of course not,' Melita said.

'Then I think God is very frightening,' Rose-Marie confided. 'He is always looking to see what we are doing and thinking we ought to be punished.'

'That is not true,' Melita said. 'I will read you a book I have brought with me from

81

England which will tell you how much God cares for everyone, even little birds. If we do make mistakes, He forgives us and forgets about them.'

'Is that true?' Rose-Marie asked.

'I promise you it is absolutely true,' Melita answered, 'for God is a kind and understanding Person who is always there to help us if we are in trouble or danger.'

She told Rose-Marie how when she was coming over from England, the storm was very bad and everyone had prayed because they thought the ship was going to the bottom of the ocean.

Soon afterwards the wind had begun to die down and the sea was less tempestuous.

'And God did that?' Rose-Marie asked.

'Yes, He did,' Melita said positively.

She saw that this had evoked a new train of thought in the child, but she was too wise to go on with the subject and instead she said:

'What have you to show me now?'

'I want you to see my friend,' Rose-Marie said. 'He is very clever and he makes me pretty dolls. I think he will have one for me now.'

'Then let us go and see it,' Melita suggested.

She thought that Rose-Marie looked surreptitiously over her shoulder and she had the idea that perhaps this friend, whoever it might be, had not the whole-hearted approval of *Madame* Boisset.

But her main objective was to gain Rose-Marie's confidence and she said nothing as the child led her towards the slave quarters.

The stone huts were built on either side of a green grass ride.

There were fourteen of them, all identical in design, and as she had noticed when she arrived there were lots of very small children playing about outside.

They were laughing and tumbling about with each other, but the moment Melita appeared they became silent and sat still, even the smallest of them staring fearfully with large dark eyes.

Rose-Marie led the way quickly to the third hut on the right-hand side.

There were no children outside this one. The door was open and without knocking she walked in.

An old woman with a deeply lined face but with shrewd penetrating eyes came from a dark corner. Rose-Marie said to her imperiously:

'I want to see Philippe, Léonore!'

'He outside, *M'mselle* Rose-Marie, other side of hut. He likes be quiet when he's working.'

'He is making me a doll?' Rose-Marie asked eagerly.

'Yes, *M'mselle.*'

'Then we will go and find him.'

She turned and would have walked from the house, but Melita stopped.

She was appalled at seeing how scanty was the furniture inside the building.

There were a number of straw palliasses on the floor almost touching each other, two or three broken chairs, a table, and against one wall there was a very primitive stove and some heavy iron cooking utensils.

It was all clean and yet, Melita thought, she had never imagined people could live in such poverty-stricken surroundings with no sign of anything individual or personal about them.

'Good morning,' she said to Léonore. 'I am *Mademoiselle* Cranleigh, the new Governess.'

At the friendliness in her voice the old woman smiled.

'You come from across the sea, *M'mselle.*'

It was a statement of fact, not a question.

'Yes, from England,' Melita answered, 'and I find that Martinique is very beautiful.'

The woman nodded.

'It good you come, very good!'

Melita did not quite know what she meant, but there was a positive note in the woman's voice which made what she said seem important.

But when Melita would have replied, Rose-

Marie pulled at her hand.

'Come, *Mademoiselle!* Come quickly!' she said. 'I want to see Philippe.'

Because she did not wish to disappoint the child Melita allowed herself to be led from the hut and around the side of it to the back where they found a boy.

He was about sixteen; he had only one leg and was sitting on the ground with a crutch at his side and a pile of leaves in front of him.

'This is Philippe,' Rose-Marie said eagerly.

The boy looked up to smile at her.

'Have you my doll ready for me, Philippe?' she asked.

He nodded and picking up something which lay on his other side held it out.

It was, Melita saw, an extremely attractive doll, about 18 inches high and apparently dressed in the most exquisitely coloured gown.

Rose-Marie took it with a cry of delight.

'That is pretty—very pretty, Philippe. Prettier than the last one you made me. I like it very much.'

She took it in both her hands, then held it out to Melita.

'Look,' she said, 'a new doll! What shall I call her?'

Melita looked at the doll closely, and to her astonishment she found that the gown was made of leaves and so was the head dress.

'Leaves!' she exclaimed. 'What a clever idea! How do you do it, Philippe?'

Philippe did not reply. He only smiled and Rose-Marie explained:

'Philippe is dumb, he cannot speak, but he understands everything you say to him.'

She spoke in a matter-of-fact tone, but for a moment Melita found it difficult to know what to say.

She looked down at what Philippe had in his hands and realised he was making another doll.

'Will you show me how you do it?' she asked. 'It is very clever of you!'

'He is clever!' Rose-Marie said proudly. 'Look, *Mademoiselle*, the face is a leaf! When he makes a doll like me he uses a white leaf, and when it is like himself he finds a brown leaf just the same colour.'

'The doll is really quite uncanny,' Melita thought.

Then as if Philippe realised she was waiting to see how he worked, he showed her first the young coconuts from which he carved the head, then the bust and finally the lower part of the body.

He fastened them all together with a long skewer which looked to Melita rather like a steel knitting-needle.

Then swiftly he took the leaves which lay beside him and began to smooth them over the doll's body, twisting them round the head and over the shoulders and holding them in place with small pins.

'I got Philippe the pins,' Rose-Marie said proudly. 'I asked Papa for them and he bought them in St. Pierre.'

Melita thought it fascinating the way the boy's dark fingers worked so skilfully and so sensitively.

The head of the doll was decorated with a leaf that looked like the brightly coloured handkerchiefs the black women wore round their heads.

Then the shoulders were draped with leaves that were green shot with red and the waist had a sash that looked like scarlet silk.

The arms were fashioned also of twisted leaves and then the full skirt was made of leaf upon leaf, like the many petticoats Melita herself wore under her muslin gown.

Philippe was so skilful and so quick with his hands that almost before it seemed possible the doll was finished and Rose-Marie gave a cry of delight.

'She is beautiful, Philippe! Is that one also for me?'

Philippe shook his head.

'No?' she pouted.

'You have one new doll,' Melita said. 'I think if Philippe had promised this one to someone else it would be greedy to expect two presents in one day.'

'Yes, of course,' Rose-Marie agreed, 'and thank you, Philippe. I love my doll very much. I will think of a special name for her.'

She looked up at Melita.

'One day, *Mademoiselle*, perhaps Philippe will make a doll that looks like you. Then we can call her 'Melita'. This one is dark, so she could not be you, could she?'

'I should be delighted if Philippe will make a doll like me,' Melita replied.

She smiled at the boy, then with Rose-Marie cuddling her new possession in her arms they walked back the way they had come.

'How long will the doll last?' Melita asked. 'The leaves must fade.'

'Sometimes two weeks, sometimes three,' Rose-Marie answered. 'When it gets dried up and rather smelly Philippe will make me another one.'

'Do you ever give Philippe a present?' Melita asked, thinking of the bare quarters in which the boy lived, and the lack of possessions in it.

Rose-Marie shook her head.

'Cousin Josephine will not let me,' she

88

answered. 'I wanted to give the slave children some of my toys, the ones I no longer play with, but she said 'No'. They were slaves and I must not spoil them.'

That was just what she would think, Melita prevented herself from saying aloud.

It was too soon, she told herself, to contradict *Madame* Boisset or try to change the orders she had given Rose-Marie.

She could understand now what the *Comte* had meant when he had said there were many things he had accepted even though he knew they were wrong.

'It is not going to be easy,' she thought to herself.

She felt suddenly afraid of *Madame* Boisset, with her aggressive voice and hard, suspicious eyes.

'Now I will show you the sugar,' Rose-Marie was saying.

They walked from the slave quarters across the grass to a tall building that stood just in front of the water-wheel which ground the sugar cane.

There appeared to be a great deal of activity going on inside and when Melita followed Rose-Marie in through the open doorway she knew she was seeing the big copper vats in which the juice of the sugar cane was boiled.

There were slaves, naked to the waist, stirring the vats. There was a strong smell of sugar while the heat from the fires over which the vats stood made the place intolerably hot.

There was the noise of many men talking to each other and continual movement which left Melita bewildered until a voice beside her said:

'Are you interested in seeing the enormous amount of work that has to be done before a piece of sugar reaches your lips?'

It was the *Comte* who spoke to her and Melita heard a mocking note in his voice, as if he was amused at how surprised and bewildered she was by everything she saw.

'Please explain it to me,' she said simply.

He paused for a moment as he looked at the slaves tending the great copper vats. Then he said:

'Sugar is the curse that afflicted the Caribbean with slavery. I expect you know that Christopher Columbus brought the sugar cane to Santa Domingo on his second voyage in 1493?'

'Yes, I did know that,' Melita answered.

'It was a success and the cultivation spread to Cuba and all the other islands. But it was a Spanish Priest who, since there was not enough local labour, conceived the idea of buying Negroes from the Portuguese in Africa and

90

shipping them to the West Indies as slaves.'

'A Priest!' Melita said beneath her breath.

She remembered the tales of cruelty, privation and torture she had heard about the treatment of the slaves.

Her father had told her how much they had suffered at the hands of the traders who carried them from their own country.

'It was the Dutch,' the *Comte* went on, 'who first taught the British cane planters in Barbados how to build the big mills to crush the cane and to boil the juice in copper vats like these you see there to crystallise it.'

'Is it difficult to do?' Melita asked.

'Not really,' the *Comte* replied, 'but the cane must be processed soon after it is cut.'

Melita watched the men at work for some moments. Then she said almost beneath her breath:

'So much suffering over the years just to make a sweet substance to put in our tea or to make jam!'

'That is true,' the *Comte* said in a serious voice, 'and it says a great deal for the spirit of these people that after centuries of hardship they can still laugh, sing, dance and hope.'

'For freedom?' Melita asked. 'Even freedom will not restore them to their native land.'

'That is true,' the *Comte* agreed.

91

At that moment as if to illustrate his words the men at work on the copper vats began to sing.

The sound they made with their deep voices was exactly, Melita thought, what she expected to hear from Negroes.

Through the steam rising from the vats and the heat in the great building she could see their white teeth gleaming and the sweat pouring from their naked chests and arms.

But their song was infectious and soon almost everybody was joining in and it seemed to rise up into the very roof.

Then almost as if someone had slammed a shutter over the sunlight the song ceased abruptly.

One after the other the Overseers bawled out orders and cracked their whips ominously.

Melita looked at the *Comte* in surprise for explanation. Then she realised that behind them in the doorway stood *Madame* Boisset!

She was wearing a red gown, a straw hat on her dark head.

'Are you encouraging these people to waste their time in singing when they should be working, Étienne?' she asked in her harsh tone.

'On the contrary,' the *Comte* said coolly, 'I have always believed that men who are happy work better and quicker than those who do it sullenly and in silence.'

'That may be your opinion, but it is not mine,' *Madame* Boisset said contemptuously.

She walked towards one of the Overseers. Melita heard her speaking to him sharply and she thought the slaves near her seemed almost to wince away as if already they felt the whip across their shoulders.

The *Comte* turned abruptly on his heel and walked out of the building.

There was a moment or so before Rose-Marie realised he had gone. Then she turned and ran after him, and Melita followed.

But they were too late.

As they left the building they saw the *Comte* about fifty yards away swing himself into the saddle of a horse that was being held by a young Negro boy.

'Papa! Papa!' Rose-Marie called. 'Wait for me!'

But already the *Comte* was riding away and the hoofs of his horse threw up behind him a cloud of dust and there was no doubt that he was in a hurry to be gone.

'And who shall blame him?' Melita asked herself.

She could understand how frustrating it was for him to have everything he said and did queried by his wife's cousin.

Why did he allow it? Surely, since he was the *Comte de* Vesonne, the plantation belonged to him?

She found herself puzzling over the *Comte* as Rose-Marie took her first to look at the water-wheel, then into the long store-house that she had seen on arrival.

There the sugar that had been processed was packed in barrels ready, Melita knew, to be carried to ships in the harbour of St. Pierre from where they would sail to markets all over the world.

'What time do the slaves start work?' Melita asked an Overseer who was supervising the slaves moving the barrels.

'At six in the morning, *M'mselle*, promptly,' he replied.

'And at what time do they stop?'

'At dusk.'

'It is a long day,' Melita remarked.

She wondered how many fell ill from overwork, but was too shy to ask more questions.

She remembered her father telling her of the terrible mortality among the slaves being carried from the coast of Africa to Brazil, the Spanish Colonies, the Caribbean and North America.

Known in the trade as 'the middle passage', no-one will ever know how many died or com-

94

mitted suicide on the voyage.

'A slave had no more than five feet six inches in length to lie on,' Sir Edward had said. 'The men were chained, two by two, by their hands and feet to rigbolts fastened to the deck.'

'How cruel, Papa!' Melita exclaimed.

'They were usually below decks for two or three days at a time. Some died of suffocation and the mortality was ten in a hundred.'

There was a great deal more to see including a monkey in a cage which Rose-Marie fed with bananas and nuts, and an aviary of parrots which Melita learnt had been caught in the forests. Their brilliant plumage, their long tails and their shrewd, unwinking eyes were fascinating.

When they had walked a little way round the large garden Melita realised that it was noon already and time for luncheon.

She took Rose-Marie back to the house and all the while she talked to the child she could not help wondering where the *Comte* had gone and if he would return for the midday meal.

They had in fact finished the first course when he came in.

He apologised to *Madame* Boisset who said sharply:

'I hope you have not wasted *your* morning, Étienne, in the same manner as your daughter

95

has. I should have thought that after all the expense and trouble of conveying a Governess here she might have settled down to working out a proper curriculum for Rose-Marie!'

Melita determined not to reply but Rose-Marie said:

'I have learnt a lot of English words this morning—sugar...doll...and...parrot!'

'Very good!' the *Comte* said. 'That is excellent, Rose-Marie! Do you think you will remember them by tomorrow morning?'

'I shall know lots more by then,' Rose-Marie said confidently.

Madame Boisset did not comment, she merely looked disagreeable. And as if she was determined to provoke the *Comte* she said after he had helped himself to the food the servants brought him:

'May I enquire, or is it indiscreet, how long we shall be honoured by your presence? As your Housekeeper, if for no other reason, I am interested to know your plans.'

'Quite frankly I have none at the moment,' the *Comte* answered. 'I have been looking round the estate. Did you realise a number of the roofs in the slave quarters are in a disgraceful condition? They are no protection against the rain and they should be repaired immediately.'

Madame Boisset gave him a smile that was full of malice.

'Have you considered how much these repairs will cost and where the money is to come from?'

'I believe, although I have not seen the figures, that the crops we have already sold this year show a good profit.'

'But we had a large deficit to make up,' *Madame* Boisset replied, 'or had you forgotten to take that into account?'

'I should like to study the books.'

Madame Boisset raised her eye-brows.

'Why this sudden interest? Your attitude is certainly different from what it has been this past year.'

'I realise that,' the *Comte* answered, 'and I am now prepared to make up for my negligence.'

'How delightful!' *Madame* Boisset sneered. 'We must study the accounts together—side by side—and of course I shall appreciate your help and support, as I have always appreciated it, if it has ever been offered me.'

Her voice was not only sarcastic, it was also full of innuendo; and Melita, looking at Rose-Marie, realised that the child had stopped eating and had gone rather pale.

This verbal duelling between *Madame* Boisset and the *Comte* was, Melita felt, having a harmful effect on her and it should not continue. She made up her mind that she would speak to the *Comte* about it.

Surely he could prevent *Madame* from being rude to him—at least in front of his daughter?

'As Rose-Marie has finished, *Madame*,' she said putting down her own spoon and fork, 'and as she has had a long morning, I think she should go upstairs and rest.'

'That is the most sensible thing I have heard you say, *Mademoiselle*,' *Madame* Boisset replied. 'Let me point out that if Rose-Marie had been in the School-Room this morning, where she should have been, she would not be so tired.'

Her voice sharpened as she went on:

'I hope that when she has had her siesta you will give her some proper lessons. I shall be interested to hear what she learns.'

Melita did not reply, she merely made *Madame* a small curtsey and helped Rose-Marie down from her chair.

The child ran impulsively towards her father and put her arms around his neck.

'I love you, Papa!' she said. 'I love you! Please stay with us.'

The *Comte* kissed his daughter, but he did

not reply to her plea.

When Melita and Rose-Marie were outside the room the child said:

'I want Papa to stay here. It is Cousin Josephine who drives him away! She quarrels with him, then Papa gets angry and goes to St. Pierre, and I am always afraid he will not come back.'

'He will always come back to you, Rose-Marie,' Melita said soothingly.

'I want him to stay with me,' Rose-Marie said almost stubbornly.

'I think he means to stay, for the moment at any rate,' Melita said, 'so do not worry about it. Try to sleep.'

She took Rose-Marie into her bed-room which was next door to her own.

It was a large, airy room, beautifully furnished, and Melita noticed that over the child's bed there was an oil painting of a young woman, not unlike Rose-Marie herself.

'Is that your mother?' she asked.

Rose-Marie nodded and said petulantly:

'God took her away from us. I hate God! He was cruel to take Mama when I wanted her.'

'You must tell me all about it another time,' Melita said. 'You are tired now.'

Eugénie appeared and started to undress Rose-Marie and Melita looked at the picture.

There was no doubt that the *Comtesse* had a very sweet face.

The picture, she thought, must have been painted when she was very young for she looked child-like and little older than Rose-Marie herself.

Her eyes were wide and trusting, and she had been portrayed by the artist in a white gown with a wide lace bertha, which revealed her sloping shoulders, while her skirts billowed out from a tiny waist.

Her hair was not black, but dark brown, similar in colour to her daughter's and curled against her oval face. Her eyes were brown too.

Melita's attention was recalled from the picture by hearing Rose-Marie say plaintively:

'I am tired—I am very tired.'

'You go to sleep, *ma petite,*' Eugénie said. 'When you wake up you will want to play with your toys.'

'I want my doll, the doll Philippe made for me.'

'I will fetch it for you,' Melita replied.

They had left the doll in the School-Room when they went down to luncheon and she knew exactly on which chair Rose-Marie had put it.

But when she reached the School-Room it was not there.

100

She looked around thinking perhaps one of the servants had tidied it away or perhaps Eugénie had put it in a cupboard, but there was no sign of it.

Finally there was nowhere else she could look and she returned to Rose-Marie's bed-room.

Rose-Marie was asleep. Eugénie put her finger to her lips and came out through the door, closing it quietly behind her.

'I cannot find the doll,' Melita said.

'*Madame* took it,' Eugénie replied.

'*Madame?* But why?'

'She not like *la petite M'mselle* visit Philippe. I would have warned you, but I not think *M'mselle* Rose-Marie go there. Big fuss last time he made her doll.'

As they were speaking Eugénie and Melita walked towards the School-Room.

Now as they entered it Melita said:

'But why? What harm can there be in that poor crippled boy making those beautiful dolls for Rose-Marie?'

'*Madame* not allow *petite M'mselle* talk with slaves! She say if Philippe well enough make dolls he work in fields.'

'But that would be impossible!' Melita exclaimed.

'He extra mouth to feed, *M'mselle. Madame* want only workers.'

101

'And the *Comte?*'

Melita could not help questioning Eugénie. There was a little pause before she replied:

'When *Monsieur* look after us very different. Then everybody happy.'

There was no need for the black woman to say any more.

Her tone was expressive and Melita could hear the Overseers crack their whips and the sudden hush that had silenced the singing voices when *Madame* had entered the sugar refinery.

Eugénie suddenly looked over her shoulder as if she thought somebody might be listening.

'*M'mselle* must be careful—very careful,' she warned, 'otherwise sent away.'

Melita drew in her breath.

She knew only too well that that was exactly what *Madame* was already planning—to send her back to England on some pretext or other.

Even if the *Comte* tried to save her from such a humiliation, she had the idea that he might be powerless.

Because she did not wish to seem to Eugénie to be prying or over-curious she went from the School-Room into her bed-room.

She realised that this was the time of day when she would be on her own, and she knew that if she was sensible she would lie down on

her bed and read one of the books she had
brought with her.

She had in fact been looking forward to
reading those that had been packed in her
trunks and which she had not had with her on
the voyage.

But because she was worried and upset by
her thoughts and apprehensive once again
about the future, she could not rest.

She moved about her small bed-room, then
decided she would go into the garden.

She thought that *Madame* would be lying
down and doubtless the *Comte* like all other
men in the tropics rested, so that no-one
would notice her if she slipped down the
stairs and out through the door which led into
the garden.

It was very hot and the sun seemed to burn
its way even through the silk of her sunshade.

She hurried across the lawn to seek the
shadow of the trees which lay beyond the
flowering shrubs where Rose-Marie had found
her frog.

Yesterday evening Melita had been too be-
mused by the *Comte* to look around her, but
now she realised that where the formal gardens
ended there was a wildness of colour and
beauty.

Everywhere there were fruit trees and now

she understood why it was called 'Vesonne-des-Arbres'.

She recognised the blossom of the avocado, the cherry and the guava, but there were others she did not know and one in particular was more beautiful than any tree she had ever seen, or could imagine.

The pink and white blossoms, instead of having oval-shaped petals, were brush-shaped rising from a cone but soft and delicate like the feathers of an Angel's wings.

It was so unusual, so lovely, that Melita stood beneath one of the trees entranced, her head thrown back to look up, the action revealing the long line of her throat.

She looked so beautiful and so ethereal, almost part of the blossom itself, that the man who was watching her stood spellbound for a moment before he came to her side.

She felt rather than saw him come and did not move.

She only stood still with her head up-turned, the sunshine making patterns on her gown and glinting like living gold on her fair hair.

'I have never seen a tree like it,' she said at length as he did not speak.

'Do you know what it is called?' the *Comte* asked.

Melita shook her head.

He raised his arm and picked several of the blossoms from the tree, then he placed them in the palm of her hand.

'They are called *Pomme d'Amour.*'

'The Apple of Love,' Melita said almost beneath her breath.

Then because she could not help herself her eyes met his, and there was no need to guess the meaning in his voice when he had said the name of the tree.

There was silence for a moment, then the *Comte* said:

'Why are you here when you should be resting?'

Melita answered truthfully.

'I wanted to think, but somehow it was...impossible to do so in the house.'

'That is what I felt too,' he said, 'and although I did not see you come here, I must have known instinctively that I would find you.'

Again their eyes met and he said:

'I feel I have some explaining to do. Let us go a little further into the shade of the trees so that no-one will find us.'

It was unnecessary to put into words who they were afraid might do so, and obediently Melita moved away under the *Pomme d'Amour,* feeling as if somehow its beauty had become a part of herself and the man walking beside her.

The *Comte* did not speak until the trees grew even thicker and the rays of the sun could barely percolate through their branches.

Then he indicated a little rise in the ground which was covered with moss. Melita sat down on it, and he lowered himself to sit beside her.

She had no need of her sunshade, and she laid it down beside her and put the blossoms of the *Pomme d'Amour* in her lap, touching them with the tips of her fingers.

'The blossoms of these trees, which are the most beautiful on the whole island, are like you,' the *Comte* said after a moment.

She felt a little quiver run through her at the depth in his voice. Then with an effort he looked away from her and said:

'I cannot allow you to remain in ignorance any longer of what is happening here at Vesonne.'

'It is so beautiful,' Melita said softly, 'the most beautiful place I have ever seen. I do not like to think that the people here...are unhappy, and as you know...it is...bad for Rose-Marie.'

She paused before she went on:

'I made up my mind this morning that I would speak to you about it: Rose-Marie is a sensitive child, and every time there is any unpleasantness she trembles and it is impossible for her to eat.'

'Do you suppose I do not realise that?' the *Comte* asked, and there was an unmistakable bitterness in his voice.

Melita looked at him and realised how attractive his profile was against the greenery around them.

He was not wearing a hat and his dark hair, thick, shiny and luxuriant, and with a slight wave in it, grew back from a square forehead.

She found herself wondering how it would feel to touch, then blushed at her own thoughts.

'When I thought it a good idea to accept your Stepmother's suggestion to employ an English Governess,' he said at length, 'I considered only my daughter and what a benefit it would be to her.'

He turned to look at Melita before he went on:

'I did not think of myself until I saw you standing on deck.'

Melita's eyes fell before the expression in his and she played with the blossom in her lap.

'The reason why I was in St. Pierre,' the *Comte* went on, 'was not only to meet you but also because I had left the plantation and sworn that I would never go back.'

'How could you do that?' she asked.

'I could stand it no longer,' he answered. 'Even in the short time you have been here, you must have realised that the position is intolerable for me.'

'But why? If the plantation bears your... name,' Melita asked in a small voice, 'why is it not...yours?'

The *Comte* gave a deep sigh.

'That is what I intend to tell you.'

Suddenly he threw himself back in the grass and clasping his hands behind his head said with his eyes closed:

'I was brought up here. I love Vesonne. It is part of my blood, and the memories of my childhood and the happiness my father and mother gave us all are unforgettable.'

Melita thought he must have been a very attractive little boy and she could understand how proud his parents must have been of him.

'My father was a bad manager,' the *Comte* went on. 'There was never very much money, and although we were happy we often had to do without things which other people would have considered essential. When I became twenty-one there was in fact a financial crisis.'

There was a look of pain on his face before he continued:

108

'My father decided the only way to keep the plantation going was for me to marry a girl with a fortune.'

The last word was spoken sharply, and Melita glanced at him, but she did not speak.

'All the arrangements were made by my father and *Monsieur* Calviare, who was to be my father-in-law,' he continued. 'I was not consulted and not until everything was a *fait accompli* did I actually meet my future wife.'

Melita knew that marriages in France were always arranged, but she could not help thinking that it was almost barbaric as the *Comte* told her of it in a voice which expressed all too vividly what he must have felt.

'I accepted the situation,' he went on, 'and if I did not look forward to my marriage with any enthusiasm I realised it was inevitable.'

He drew in his breath.

'I wanted to be gay. I had tasted the delights of Paris, and enjoyed myself in St. Pierre. I had no wish to settle down.'

'You were very...young,' Melita murmured.

'And, although you may not believe me, very idealistic,' the *Comte* replied.

He looked up at her as she sat a little stiffly beside him, her back straight, her head bent over the blossoms in her lap.

'I had always imagined that one day I would

109

fall in love, one day I would find a woman who would embody all the ideals that I kept secretly in my heart. Then I would ask her to be my wife.'

'I can...understand...that.'

'But naturally,' he went on in a different voice, 'I had to do what my father asked of me. And Cécile was very sweet and very pretty.'

There was silence before he said:

'Two things I did not realise until I was married. First was that Cécile had never grown up. She was a child, an attractive, delightful child, but she was not a woman, and secondly, that the most powerful influence in her life had been her Cousin Josephine.'

At the mention of *Madame* Boisset's name, Melita felt almost as if a shadow blocked out the sunshine.

'Josephine was not at home when I married,' the *Comte* went on, 'because she was already the wife of *Monsieur* Boisset, who lived near Fort de France.

'The family continually spoke of her and I learnt that she was an orphan who had been brought up by *Monsieur* and *Madame* Calviare as if she was their own daughter.'

He moved restlessly before he continued:

'She was twelve years older than her Cousin, and it was, of course, understandable that

Cécile should admire the older girl and try to emulate her in every way.'

His lips met in a tight line. Then he forced himself to go on:

'But that did not concern me because Josephine had her own home and Cécile and I came to live at Vesonne.'

Melita made a little movement. Somehow— she could not think why—it hurt to think of him bringing his bride back to his home.

'Shortly after our marriage my father and mother retired to St. Pierre,' the *Comte* continued. 'He had always found the work on the plantation too much for him and he was content that I should take over his responsibilities and try to restore the estate to its former prosperity.'

'You could...afford to do that?' Melita asked.

'Cécile was a great heiress,' the *Comte* replied, 'but *Monsieur* Calviare was a business man and he made one stipulation. Although he gave us a large sum of money to put the plantation in order, repair and redecorate the house, and pay for a thousand other things that wanted doing, he insisted that Cécile's money remained her own.'

Melita glanced at the *Comte*. She was beginning to understand what he was telling her.

'Of course, under French law a woman's fortune becomes her husband's on marriage,' the *Comte* said, 'and although I had control over Cécile's income once she was my wife, there was one proviso.'

'What was...that?'

'Her capital was hers and remained in her name. *Monsieur* Calviare also made certain that the money he would leave on his death would be hers.'

Melita waited for the inevitable conclusion.

'When he died he left Cécile a huge fortune and we spent it gaily. She never at any time during our married life ever made me feel that the money was not mine.'

The *Comte* sighed again.

'She was a child—a child who smiled if you smiled at her, and who could cry as easily as the spring rains fall from the skies. She never questioned any action I took or any order I gave, and I can say quite truthfully that I made her happy.'

'I am sure you did,' Melita said, feeling somehow she must re-assure him.

She thought at the same time that what he left unsaid was very obvious.

He was an intelligent, clever man who had been married to an immature girl who might give him laughter, but could give him nothing else.

'Then Josephine was widowed,' the *Comte* said as if he sounded a knell of sudden doom. 'She was left very little money. Her husband who had seemed to be well-to-do had many impecunious relatives so she came to stay with us at Vesonne!'

Now there was no mistaking the darkness in his expression and in the tone of his voice.

'At first I welcomed her,' he said; 'she was a companion for Cécile and she took over the running of the household which had not been satisfactory. Then gradually I realised that two things were happening.'

There were silence until Melita prompted: 'What were...they?'

'First that Josephine had complete ascendancy over my wife,' the *Comte* said. 'Secondly, that she was in love with me!'

It was what Melita had expected to hear, and yet somehow it was a blow when he actually put it into words.

'What...did you...do?'

'It made me extremely uncomfortable,' he answered. 'I suggested to Cécile that she should send her away, but she burst into tears at the thought and clung to Josephine as I realised she had clung to her when she had been a child.'

'What...happened?'

'I was so busy that I left the problem to solve

itself,' the *Comte* answered. 'I was working all hours of the day on the plantation, cultivating land, bringing in the different crops, making contracts for sales and taking the sugar, the fruits and the coffee to the ships to see that they were properly stowed away so that they did not deteriorate on the voyage.'

Just for a moment there was a note of elation in his voice as if the work had been enjoyable.

Then he said dully:

'Quite suddenly, without any explanation as to why it should happen, Cécile died!'

'But how?' Melita asked.

The *Comte* sat up, put his arms around his knees and stared ahead of him.

'Even now I can hardly credit that it happened,' he said. 'I went to St. Pierre with a special shipment of sugar which I had sold to Holland. I was away perhaps ten days. I returned to find that Cécile was dead, and even the Doctor had no explanation for her sudden death.'

'There must have been...one,' Melita insisted.

'If there was, I did not receive it,' the *Comte* replied. 'Josephine said Cécile had been ailing, and complaining of head-aches and pains in her stomach. But she had thought it was just a

114

slight fever or indigestion and had not sent for the Doctor until it was too late.'

'How terrible!' Melita said.

'As you can imagine I was stunned,' the *Comte* replied, 'but when the funeral was over Josephine produced Cécile's will.'

Melita waited, now there was no reason to ask a question.

'When we were married and *Monsieur* Calviare had insisted that Cécile must retain her own fortune, we had both made wills in each other's favour. I had left all my possessions to Cécile and to any children there might be of the marriage, and she had left all her money to me, unconditionally.'

'And this had been...changed?' Melita asked knowing the answer was obvious.

'Cécile had made another will without my knowledge in which she left all her money to Josephine for her life-time.'

The *Comte* drew in his breath before he finished:

'The only thing that could break this bequest was if I married Josephine, in which case the money would become mine.'

Melita bit back the exclamation which rose to her lips.

After a moment she managed to say:

'The will was...valid?'

'Completely valid. It had been witnessed by the Priest who comes to the plantation to say Mass and by another Frenchman of some standing who happened to be travelling in the vicinity.'

'*Madame* Boisset must have...contrived it.'

'Of course she contrived it,' the *Comte* said harshly. 'I told you that she dominated Cécile absolutely, mind, body and soul, and when I was away she must have persuaded my wife to sign that monstrous document which was couched in phrases which Cécile herself would never have used.'

'But surely you could prove that?'

'How?' the *Comte* asked. 'Do you suppose I have not taken legal advice on the matter— of course I have! I consulted the best Attorney in the whole of St. Pierre. Do you know what he said to me?'

'What did he say?' Melita asked.

'He was a Frenchman. He said: "My dear boy, but you must marry your wife's cousin. Why not? All women are alike in the dark!"'

Melita was very still, then she said:

'I am sorry...more sorry than I can...possibly say.'

'There is no reason for me to worry you with my troubles,' the *Comte* said almost roughly.

Then he turned his head to look at her and added:

'That is not true! There is every reason. You must know why I wished to tell you this. Why I had to tell you! But only God knows what I can do about it.'

CHAPTER FOUR

Melita could not reply. Any words she might have uttered were strangled in her throat.

At the same time because of the deep, passionate note in the *Comte's* voice she experienced a sudden feeling of inescapable joy sweep over her.

Then, as if it was impossible for him to remain still, the *Comte* rose to his feet and walked from the bank on which they had been sitting towards the nearest tree. He stood with his hand against the trunk as if he needed its support.

Then with his back to her he said:

'It is too soon. I had intended to wait before I said anything to you, but it is impossible!'

Melita looked at him but she did not move or speak and he went on:

'The moment I saw you as I walked across the deck was as if you were enveloped with a white light and I knew absolutely and completely in the passing of a second what had happened.'

In the silence which seemed to be part of the

118

beauty of the *Pomme d'Amour* blossoms above them Melita said almost in a whisper:

'What did you...know?'

The *Comte* turned then to look at her.

'I knew,' he said slowly, 'that you were what I had been seeking all my life, yearning for, needing, but which I had never found because—you were not there.'

She looked up at him and as their eyes met she felt as if her heart turned over in her breast. Then she said, still in a whisper:

'How could...you be so...sure?'

'I was sure then, and I knew it for an absolute certainty when we had luncheon together,' he replied. 'Already you were a part of me, your thoughts were my thoughts, your mind was my mind, and my heart was yours.'

Melita remembered how surprised she had been that he seemed to know what she was thinking and anticipate what she was about to say.

She knew too that he was expressing what she also had felt since she had first seen him and which she had known with absolute surety when she had gone into the garden the previous night. She had been drawn like a magnet towards his voice even before she saw him.

'Do you mean,' she asked hesitatingly, 'that

119

you...love me?'

The *Comte* smiled.

'Love?' he questioned. 'It is such an inadequate word to describe what I feel and what you mean to me. You are mine, Melita, mine although I have not even touched you, mine although for the moment I dare not ask you to marry me.'

She was trembling as he went on:

'But you are my woman, my real wife! Mine because our souls have met across eternity and we have found each other after who knows how many centuries of seeking?'

Melita clasped her fingers together.

Everything he was saying to her was so moving and at the same time it seemed so absolutely right and true that she herself might also be saying the same words.

For a long moment the *Comte* stood looking at her. Then he said very quietly:

'Come here, Melita!'

She rose to her feet while he did not move.

Step by step she crossed the soft grass until she was standing just in front of him, beneath the overhanging branches of the petal-laden trees.

'You are so lovely,' he said, 'so unbelievably beautiful, but it is not only your beauty which draws me, my darling, but your mind, your spirit and your heart which I knew belonged to me from the first moment I looked into your eyes.'

He drew a deep breath.

'I have nothing to offer you—nothing! And yet I feel that everything else except ourselves and our love is unimportant. Am I right?'

Now there was a hint of anxiety in his voice and in the expression in his eyes.

He made no movements to touch her, and yet she felt that irresistibly he drew her to him and she was already close in his arms.

She knew he was waiting for her answer, and after a moment, in a voice he could hardly hear, she spoke.

'I love...you!'

They stood looking at each other and it seemed as if the whole world stood still. Then very gently as if she was one of the pink and white blossoms on the tree above them, the *Comte* put his arms around her.

For a moment he did not kiss her, he simply put his cheek against hers and held her close.

'Melita! Melita!' he murmured. 'Is this true? Tell me it is not a dream from which we shall both awaken?'

'It is true,' she repeated almost as if she spoke to a child who wanted to be reassured.

'I love you!' he said. 'I love you overwhelm-

121

ingly and I swear that I have never in my whole life felt like this before.'

There was something very solemn in the way he spoke and still he stood with his cheek against hers, his arms enveloping her, before he said almost as if he spoke to himself:

'Am I being unfair? You are very young, my precious, and I am much older than you. God knows I want to protect and take care of you. I am so afraid of harming you.'

'I have never felt so...secure...so safe, or so...happy since Papa...died,' Melita murmured.

The Comte raised his head.

'Is that true—really true?'

'I have been so...afraid,' she answered, 'very afraid of being...alone, of not knowing what to...do or who I could turn to...and now there is...you.'

As she said the last word there was a sudden light in her eyes and a radiance in her face that the *Comte* could not misunderstand.

Then as if he could not help himself he drew her closer still and his lips found hers.

Melita had never been kissed before and for a moment she felt shy and a little uncertain.

Then as the *Comte's* mouth held her captive she felt a sudden streak of sunlight run through her.

It evoked a sensation so wonderful, so rapturous, so unlike anything she had ever known before, that she knew it was part of the perfection of the Divine.

She felt as if her body melted into the *Comte's* and they became one person.

She knew too that the beauty, the wonder and the ecstasy he aroused in her was what he was feeling himself.

It was all part of the sunshine, the blossom on the trees, and the fragrance of the flowers.

'This is love...this is life!' Melita thought.

Then she found it was impossible to think, but only feel a glory she had not known existed.

How long the kiss lasted she had no idea, she only knew that when at length the *Comte* took his lips from hers she laid her head weakly against his shoulder and shut her eyes.

She felt that what she had experienced had left her depleted of everything except a wonder which came from Heaven itself.

'I love you, *ma belle,*' the *Comte* said. 'I love you until there is nothing in the world but you!'

He looked down at her face, at her long lashes dark against the whiteness of her skin.

'But we have to think, my precious one. I have to find some solution to the problem which besets me, and because it concerns you and our happiness I swear I will find the answer, however difficult it may be.'

Melita opened her eyes.

'There must...be one,' she said softly.

'There *will* be one,' the *Comte* said almost fiercely.

Her lips were near to his and he would have kissed her again. Then deliberately he looked away from her even while he still held her close in his arms.

'This is my land, my house, my home,' he said. 'But how can I keep it going? How can I even pay the everyday expenses without money?'

Although Melita thought it was the hardest thing she had ever done in her life she deliberately withdrew herself from his arms and faced him.

'It would not matter being...poor,' she said, 'if we were...together.'

'Are you sure?' the *Comte* asked.

'You know I am,' she answered, 'and I cannot help feeling that somehow, if we work very hard, perhaps cultivating less land to start with, we could make enough, at least to keep ourselves alive.'

'Do you mean that? Oh, my darling, do you really mean that?' the *Comte* asked.

'I mean it,' Melita answered. 'I am very ignorant about such matters but could you not obtain a loan...as Papa used to do, perhaps to...tide you over until you could pay the money back from your crops?'

She was standing beside the *Comte*, but he had not attempted to touch her since she had moved from the shelter of his arms.

Now he reached out and took her hand in his.

'Could anybody be more perfect or indeed more sensible?' he asked.

He kissed the back of her hand. Then he turned it over and kissed the palm, his lips making thrills ripple through her until, as her breath came quickly, he drew her once again close against him.

'I excite you,' he said. 'Oh, my love, tell me that I excite you a little as you excite me to madness?'

There was no need for Melita to answer and it was impossible for her to do so, because the *Comte* was kissing her again wildly and passionately.

Yet at the same time there was something spiritual in his kiss that made her know that their love came from God.

'We will find the answer,' he said.

Although he spoke resolutely his voice was a little unsteady, and she saw a glint of fire in his eyes.

125

'We will find it...together,' she whispered. 'Let me help you...I want to help you.'

'Do you think I could do without you?' he asked. 'This is what I have always missed—a woman with whom I could share my difficulties and problems.'

'I want to share...everything with you.'

He gave a deep sigh as if some of the pain and unhappiness left his body. Then he said:

'I told you that I had a feeling that your arrival was a momentous step not only for you but also for me. The day after tomorrow there will be two wagon-loads of sugar going to St. Pierre. I will go with them and I will visit the Bank and see if, as you suggest, they will give me a loan.'

As if the reason he needed money recalled Melita to her responsibilities, she said:

'I think...I should go...back to the...house.'

'Perhaps it would be wise,' the *Comte* agreed. 'There must be as little unpleasantness as possible, for you at any rate, until we have the answer to anything that might be said.'

They both knew of whom he was speaking and Melita felt as if the shadow of *Madame* Boisset encroached upon their happiness.

Once again she drew herself from his arms.

'I will see you tomorrow,' the *Comte* said, 'but I intend to leave very early in the morn-

126

ing to inspect the farthest point of the Estate where I believe things have been neglected for some time.'

'I wish I could come with you,' Melita said with a wistful little smile.

'One day,' the *Comte* said, almost as if he spoke prophetically, 'we will ride everywhere, side by side, and the first thing we will restore to the people who work for us is happiness.'

He saw how much his words pleased her. Then he said:

'Go back to the house, my precious love. We must be careful at dinner that we do not give ourselves away, but soon, very soon, we will be together and nothing shall ever separate us again.'

'You are in my...heart,' Melita whispered, 'as you will be in my...prayers.'

She turned away as she spoke and resolutely did not look back until she was clear of the fruit trees and on the edge of the lawn.

When she reached the shrubs with their crimson blossoms and found the little stream where Rose-Marie searched for frogs, she thought perhaps it would be unwise, in case anyone was watching from the windows, for them to see the direction from which she had come.

So she turned and walked towards the left,

climbing a little higher up the hill on which the house was built, until having reached the highest point she came down towards it.

To get to the garden door by which she had left she had to pass the part of the house where the kitchens were situated.

There was the chatter of voices and laughter from the young black girls who cleaned the house.

Melita moved past the windows and as she did so she saw there was a large bin filled with refuse waiting, she supposed, to be collected and taken away to be burnt in some other part of the Estate.

As she drew level with it she saw something lying on top of the bin, something she recognised.

It was the doll that Philippe had made for Rose-Marie lying amongst the rinds of the pawpaw, the skins of the bananas and a dark soggy mass of tea-leaves.

'How could *Madame* be so unkind to the child?' she thought.

Then looking again she drew in her breath, for the doll was not only thrown away but had been deliberately torn to shreds.

The pretty, bright-coloured leaves which formed the skirt had been ripped into shreds, the handkerchief which had covered the hair

128

torn, and the head half pulled from the coconut body.

It was deliberate destruction and Melita remembered how pretty the doll had looked and how delighted Rose-Marie had been with it.

She felt almost as if something live had been murdered.

'How could anyone be so petty, so unnecessarily destructive?' she asked herself.

The action seemed, in fact, almost abnormally vindictive.

* * * *

Her doll was the first thing Rose-Marie asked for when she awoke from her afternoon sleep.

No-one, Melita found to her relief, had noticed her absence, not even Eugénie, who, she realised, had also enjoyed a siesta.

'Did you find my doll, *Mademoiselle?*' Rose-Marie asked as Eugénie dressed her in a white muslin gown and combed her hair.

'I am afraid not,' Melita replied.

'But I left her in the School-Room, on a chair.'

'Yes, I know,' Melita agreed, 'but I think your Cousin did not wish you to keep it.'

'But Philippe made it especially for me,' Rose-Marie cried, 'and I know Papa would have let me have it. I shall tell him to make Cousin Josephine give it back to me.'

'Suppose you come and see the things I had in my trunk?' Melita suggested. 'There is a pretty little handkerchief sachet, all edged with lace. I thought we might embroider your initials on it and you can keep it on your dressing-table with your handkerchiefs in it.'

'I would like that!' Rose-Marie cried.

Melita had managed to divert her attention from the doll, but when she had her supper she began to think about it again.

'Where is Papa?' she asked. 'I want to tell Papa about my doll.'

'I think he is out on the plantation,' Melita answered. 'As you know, Rose-Marie, there is a lot of work to be done at this time of the year.'

'Cousin Josephine runs the plantation,' Rose-Marie answered. 'It upsets Papa and that is why he went to St. Pierre.'

Melita could not help smiling.

Rose-Marie was too intelligent a child, she thought, not to realise what was happening, and feel the turbulent emotions around her.

'Perhaps your Papa will be back before you are asleep,' she said consolingly.

'You will tell him to come and say good-night to me?'

'I will tell him,' Melita promised.

She tucked Rose-Marie up. Then the child put her arms round Melita's neck and pulled her head down to hers.

'I love having you here, *Mademoiselle*. It is much more fun since you arrived.'

'I am glad about that,' Melita said.

Rose-Marie kissed her cheek.

'You will not go away, will you?' she asked. 'Everyone I love goes away, then I am left only with Cousin Josephine.'

Melita felt her heart contract at the pathos in the words.

Rose-Marie, having lost her mother, was now afraid she might lose her father; there was nothing stable in her small life.

'I will stay, Rose-Marie,' she answered. 'I will not go away.'

She felt it was a promise not only to the child but also to the *Comte*.

Somehow they would win through. It would be difficult. They might have to endure hardship and perhaps many heartbreaks, but at least they would be together.

'That,' Melita told herself, 'is all that matters.'

Rose-Marie pulled her a little closer.

'If you stay I will be very good,' she said,

'and when Philippe makes me another doll, we will hide it so that Cousin Josephine will never find it.'

'We will think about that,' Melita said, feeling that she must not intrigue openly against *Madame* Boisset.

She kissed Rose-Marie and knew the child was satisfied.

She left the bed-room door open, and when she went to her own room next door she left that open too.

'When I hear the *Comte* return,' she thought, 'I will tell him that his daughter needs him.'

But actually Rose-Marie was fast asleep and it was nearly dinner time before she heard the *Comte* come up the uncarpeted stairs and walk along the landing to his own room at the far end.

It was too late, Melita thought then, to speak to him; instead she concentrated on making herself look as attractive as possible for when she met him at dinner.

She was wise enough to choose not an elaborate gown but a very simple one in case she should offend *Madame* Boisset.

But the plain muslin could not disguise the curves of her breast or the tininess of her waist.

It also threw into prominence the clarity of her pink and white skin and made the gold of her hair seem even more startling than a more elaborate gown might have done.

When she came down to the Salon she was tinglingly aware of the *Comte* as she knew he was of her, even though he merely said politely:

'*Bonsoir, Mademoiselle.*'

'*Bonsoir, Monsieur.*'

He did not look at her and she did not look at him.

'I hope, *Mademoiselle,* you have given Rose-Marie some proper lessons this afternoon?' *Madame* Boisset said tartly.

'Oh, yes, *Madame,*' Melita replied. 'We have done a little history, and we have looked up in an atlas the position of Martinique as regards the rest of the world. It was quite a comprehensive geography lesson for a small girl.'

'Tomorrow you must concentrate on arithmetic,' *Madame* Boisset said. 'The sooner Rose-Marie understands the value of money the better! It is an instinct that is lamentably lacking in some of her relatives.'

She glanced at the *Comte* as she spoke, and Melita thought uncomfortably that they were in for a meal in which everything *Madame* Boisset said would have a barbed and unpleasant meaning.

She was not mistaken.

Although the food was excellent and Melita fancied the Chef had excelled himself in an effort to please the *Comte*, everything was spoilt by the fact that *Madame* Boisset was obscurely offensive in everything she said to her, and to the *Comte* she was openly hostile.

Only when they moved into the Salon after dinner and Melita was wondering whether it would be correct for her to withdraw immediately did the *Comte* say:

'I am planning tomorrow to visit our land near Ajoupa Bouillon. I understand you have not been there for some time?'

'No,' *Madame* Boisset replied abruptly.

Then she added in a different tone of voice:

'Are you really taking an interest in the estate, Étienne? If so, there are several matters I would like to discuss with you.'

'I would be interested to hear them.'

Madame Boisset looked at the *Comte* as if she could hardly believe what she had heard. Then she turned towards Melita and said sharply:

'You may withdraw, *Mademoiselle*. I shall not need to see you again this evening.'

Melita curtsied.

'*Bonsoir, Madame. Bonsoir, Monsieur.*'

The *Comte* bowed, but he did not speak, and Melita knew that he was fighting an inclination to tell *Madame* Boisset not to address her in

134

such a rude manner.

She closed the door behind her and almost fearfully, as if she might overhear what was being said between them, she ran up the stairs to her own room.

As soon as they were alone *Madame* Boisset turned towards the *Comte*.

'You have come back, Étienne?' she asked. 'Do you really mean to stay?'

'I hope I shall be able to,' the *Comte* replied gravely.

'You know that is what I want,' *Madame* Boisset said, 'and the first thing we must do, if you intend to honour me with your presence, is to be rid of that milk-faced girl! She is quite useless. Send her back to England and the quicker the better!'

'I have no intention of doing that,' the *Comte* answered. 'I brought her here to be with Rose-Marie, and I think she will not only teach my daughter in the way I wish her to be taught, but also will have an excellent influence upon her.'

'Suggesting that mine is the opposite!'

'I did not say so, Josephine,' the *Comte* replied. 'But you have many other matters to occupy you, and I think that a young person like *Mademoiselle* Cranleigh with new interests and ideas is exactly what Rose-Marie needs.'

135

'You know that I am prepared to look after Rose-Marie as if she were my own child,' *Madame* Boisset said, 'and what she really needs, as you well know, Étienne, is brothers and sisters.'

She took a step towards the *Comte* as she spoke, then she said in a voice vibrant with emotion:

'Marry me, Étienne. Marry me and I will give you other children, a son to carry on the name, and you will have all the money you need with which to improve the Estate.'

The *Comte* gave a deep sigh and walked across the room to stand at the window looking up at the darkening sky.

'We have been through all this before, Josephine.'

'Yes, we have talked about it before,' *Madame* Boisset agreed, 'but all the talk, prevarication and delay do not make you any richer.'

The *Comte* did not answer and she went on:

'That house of yours in St. Pierre is crumbling into decay. You can have all the money you need to do it up and we can go there whenever you become bored with being here.

'We could go abroad, to Paris, to any part of Europe, to the United States, to South America, if it pleases you. Why must you be so perverse? Why must you continue to fight me when in the end you will give in simply because you have no alternative?'

'I do not wish to discuss the subject of marriage,' the *Comte* said.

'Then if you will not marry me,' *Madame* Boisset said in a voice which told him she was losing her temper, 'why should I go on feeding you, your child, your fancy Governess—or the slaves, for that matter?'

In a rising tone she continued:

'If I left and took my money with me, what do you suppose you would eat? Bananas? Because there would be very little else.'

'I think we would manage.'

Madame Boisset laughed scornfully.

'Do you know how much this place costs to run? Do you know how much the food for the slaves alone costs every year? Or have you forgotten while you idled away your days in St. Pierre that money is a necessity, even though you chose to pretend you are not interested in it.'

'I had not forgotten,' the *Comte* said quietly.

'Then marry me, Étienne. Marry me because I love you! I have always loved you! Cécile meant us to marry, you know she did.'

'Let us leave Cécile out of this,' the *Comte* said harshly.

137

'Why should I?' *Madame* Boisset demanded. 'She loved me—she loved you, too, and she wanted us to be married. Stop being a fool, Étienne, and face facts. You cannot manage without me.'

'I am sorry, Josephine,' the *Comte* said wearily. 'I hoped we could discuss matters without inevitably returning to the subject of marriage.'

'Then if you are not prepared to pay your way you can get out and stay out!' *Madame* Boisset said furiously. 'And take that woman with you! I cannot bear to see her smug English face.'

The *Comte* would have retorted angrily, but with an effort he managed to say:

'I think we would be wise to postpone this discussion for another time, Josephine. I am leaving early in the morning and tomorrow evening when I return I shall undoubtedly be tired. The following day I am going to St. Pierre.'

'To stay?'

The question was sharp.

'No. I shall come back,' the *Comte* answered. 'Then, after I have returned, we must have a sensible discussion about the future. I am very conscious, Josephine, that we cannot drift along as we have been doing in the past.'

He looked at her as he spoke and saw a sudden hope in her eyes that after all he might be capitulating to her desires.

Because he did not wish to make trouble for Melita while he was away he said again gravely and very quietly:

'Let us leave everything until the week-end. There will be time then to talk over many things.'

'Yes, of course, Étienne.'

Madame Boisset moved towards him and put her hand on his arm.

'I love you, Étienne—I love you! Kiss me! Make love to me as you have made love to so many other women, and let me show you what we can mean to each other.'

There was an emotional intensity in her words which made it sound almost as though she hissed them at him, and the *Comte* resisted the impulse to shake himself free of her restraining hand.

With an effort he managed to lift it quietly from his arm to his lips and to say as he kissed it perfunctorily:

'Forget all these problems for the moment, Josephine. I have already said, we will talk about them when I return.'

He bowed and although she would have reached out her hands towards him again he moved quickly from the room. She heard him cross the hall and open the door into the garden, then close it behind him.

She stood staring after him, before she said gloatingly:

'I have won! He is giving in because he can do nothing else!'

She turned with a flurry of her full skirts to stare at herself in the big gilt-framed mirror which stood at the end of the Salon.

For a moment she saw her own dark, triumphant eyes, then almost as if a picture was superimposed upon it she saw a head of golden hair, a white skin and a pair of softly curving lips.

Her eyes narrowed.

★ ★ ★ ★

Melita found it impossible to sleep.

It was a very hot night and the breeze which usually came at sunset had died away to leave the air almost stifling.

She had a feeling there might be a thunderstorm later. In the meantime she tossed and turned and finally rose to walk to the window to look out. The moon was rising in the clear sky with the stars glittering like diamonds beside it.

Now there was only silence where in the

daytime there was always the distant babble of voices, the songs of the slaves, or the creak of the water-mill.

What had happened after she had come to bed? Melita wondered. Her thoughts shied away from thinking of the *Comte* and *Madame* Boisset together.

Instead she recalled the wonder when he had held her in his arms beneath the *Pomme d'Amour* and she had known an ecstasy that was not of this world.

How perfect it had been, how wonderful!

She felt as if her heart called to him. Then almost as if she heard her own heart-beat there was a sound which she could not at first identify.

It seemed to come not from the darkness of the garden but from within herself.

She thought she must be imagining it, and she moved from the window which overlooked the garden in front of the house, to one at the side of the room.

From here she looked out over the plantation towards the sea, and now unmistakably she realised that she had heard not her own heart but the beat of a drum which sounded as if it came from far away.

She listened but it was so soft that she thought she must have imagined it, and then again it was there.

'Come to me! Come to me!' it seemed to be repeating over and over again so that Melita found herself saying the words first in French, then in English.

'*Venez à moi.* Come to me. *Venez à moi.*'

A drum, she decided finally, but why?

It drew her.

She listened and had an irresistible craving to obey the sound it made.

She went on listening and finally, because the rhythm of it seemed to beat not only in her mind but in every nerve of her body, she knew she must find out what is was.

She had no sense of fear as she put on a satin dressing-gown that she had worn in England but which had proved to be too warm for Martinique.

With her feet in heel-less slippers she opened the door of her room.

Here it was impossible for her to hear the drum, and yet the message it conveyed still held her captive.

Very, very carefully, almost without a sound, she crept down the stairs.

The garden door was not locked, only bolted, and it was easy to pull back the bolts to feel the night air on her cheeks.

Now outside she could hear the drum clearly

142

and without really considering what she was doing she walked across the lawn and down into the orchard where she had been with the *Comte* in the afternoon.

Out of sight of the house she turned left.

The silver moonlight was casting an ethereal, unearthly beauty over the fruit trees, making it easy for Melita to see her way between them. She moved downhill until they grew more dense and were interspersed with tropical plants and pine trees.

Now the drum was growing louder and still louder.

One two, *three*—one two, *three*—Come to *me*. Before the last beat was a quivering, hypnotic second of suspense. It was unmistakably primitive, entrancing, hollow, haunting!

Finally Melita could hear it very clearly as she came up against what appeared to be a fence of hibiscus shrubs.

She hesitated, then she realised that the drum was beating straight ahead of her.

She moved into the hedge itself, pushing her way slowly between the green leaves until she saw a light and, a moment later, through the branches which veiled her from sight, found what she sought.

There were a dozen Negroes sitting in a circle in a small clearing that was surrounded entirely with bushes.

The light that Melita had seen came from four candles set in the ground and in front of them there was seated Léonore, the old woman she had met when she and Rose-Marie went to find Philippe.

In front of Léonore there were several bowls and beside her a Negro was beating a small drum. As Melita stared the drumming seemed to grow into an exotic cadence.

There was a sepulchral throb to its rhythm and she realised that the Negroes' bodies were vibrating to the sound of it.

They moved almost imperceptibly with a beatific expression on their faces, while Léonore swayed backwards and forwards with her eyes shut.

Beside the vessels in front of her Melita could see what she at first thought was a crumpled white cloth lying on the ground.

Then as her eyes grew accustomed to the flickering light of the candles she saw it was not a cloth but the body of a bird.

She looked closer and saw it was dead cock, its spurs shining in the candlelight.

Then she understood and realised with a sudden constriction of her heart that what she was seeing was Voodoo!

These Negroes were engaged in Voodoo, a

religion they had brought with them from Africa, a religion that she had always known was to be found in Martinique.

She had been told of their meetings with the spirits but she had never expected to see one for herself. Yet here it was—happening in front of her very eyes.

The beat of the drum now changed and Léonore began to speak.

She was calling, in a language Melita did not understand, to Yemanjá. Melita had an idea that she had once read Yemanjá was a goddess of Voodoo.

'Yemanjá! Yemanjá!' Léonore moaned.

There was a soft murmur from the swaying bodies on either side of her.

She called again in a voice that seemed to be pleading with Yemanjá for assistance.

Then, as she held out both her hands, Philippe, who was seated near her, bent forward and put something into them.

It was a doll.

Melita could see it quite clearly, a doll dressed in leaves—red leaves. A doll with a white face and dark hair.

Melita held her breath.

There was no mistaking who was personified by the doll, and now, holding it in both hands and lifting it into the air, Léonore cried again:

145

'Yemanjá! Yemanjá!'

The drum seemed to echo her voice. Then suddenly, quite clearly and distinctly, Léonore cried:

'Save Étienne! Save him!'

She spoke not in the voice she had used before but in the voice of a young girl, a high, child-like voice, and the words were spoken in perfect French!

For a moment Melita held her breath.

Then, beset with fear that she could not control, she turned and ran away from what she had seen.

She ran back through the fruit trees, finding her way instinctively because she was past thinking, back to the security of the house.

She was breathless by the time she reached the garden door and stood for a moment holding on to it, trying to control her panic, to think herself back into a state of common sense.

It was Voodoo, she told herself, but what of it?

They had sacrificed a cock and Léonore had spoken in a strange voice.

Many unusual things could happen when people, either white or black, were in a state of trance.

That sounded quite reasonable, but as Melita crept upstairs and into the sanctuary of her own

146

room she knew that the explanation she sought was not to be found.

How could Léonore, with whom she had spoken in the slave quarters, an old, withered woman who she suspected was Philippe's grandmother, speak like a young girl in a French accent which might have been used by the *Comte* or—Melita drew in her breath—his dead wife, Cécile?

She faced then the truth.

Léonore was the Priestess or *Mambo* of Voodoo and had been possessed; but by what or whom? *A loa*, a spirit of the dead?

That was what they had called on their goddess Yemanjá to bring them.

The sacrifice of the dead cock and the sacred vessels were all part of the ritual which brought the dead back to life.

Shivering, Melita got into bed, but the picture of what she had seen, the cadence of the drum, the movement of the black bodies, the voice of Léonore when she spoke as if she were a young girl, she could not erase from her mind.

Over and over again Melita reconstructed what had happened, and everything she had ever heard or read about Voodoo came to her mind, even though she tried to disbelieve what had happened.

The *Mambo* had evoked the gods and been possessed for the moment by a *loa*. The participants in the ceremony would believe, even though Melita tried not to believe, it was the spirit of Cécile.

When they had confronted her with the likeness of *Madame* Boisset in the shape of the doll, she called out to them to save Étienne, the husband she had loved.

'It cannot be true, I dreamt it,' Melita told herself.

But even as she protested she knew that no amount of scepticism could make her doubt her own senses and her own eyes.

She longed to find the *Comte* and tell him what she had seen. Then she wondered whether he would laugh at her for being credulous, but was sure he would not.

He would understand.

He knew these people and loved them, and while he had spoken of the gods dwelling on the mountains of Martinique, he would be well aware that there were many strange gods in the forests.

The slaves, while they gave lip-service to the religion and the God of their owners, instinctively worshipped those gods they had brought with them from their own land.

Voodoo!

Even the name seemed frightening. Then Melita asked herself sternly:

'What harm can such ceremonies do to anyone?'

It was better to believe in any god rather than none—her father had said so often enough—and Voodoo made those poor servile people happy who had little else in their lives.

Perhaps it was only fair that possessing so little personally they should be compensated by experiencing a spiritual comfort and power greater than their physical subjugation.

Yet even that, Melita thought, did not explain how she had heard a young girl's voice come from between Léonore's withered old lips.

'Save Étienne! Save him!'

The sound was still echoing in her ears, and because she was frightened she began to pray prayers that had been familiar to her since her childhood.

While they gradually comforted her, the question still remained.

Why must Étienne be saved? And from whom or what?

CHAPTER FIVE

Melita was awoken by Eugénie coming into her room and saying urgently:

'*M'mselle! M'mselle!*'

She started and realised that she had dropped off to sleep again after being called by Jeanne.

It was not until long after dawn that she had fallen into a fitful slumber in which she found herself dreaming of Léonore and the drum.

Now, heavy-eyed, she stared at Eugénie and asked in a drowsy voice:

'What is the...time?'

Before Eugénie could answer, she sat up quickly, saying:

'I have overslept! Oh, I am sorry! I must get up at once!'

'Trouble, *M'mselle*. Bad trouble!' Eugénie said.

'What has happened?' Melita asked.

Eugénie burst into a flood of explanation in her broken French which was difficult to understand, until finally in horror Melita realised what had occurred.

150

Rose-Marie had awakened very early to go into the School-Room in her nightgown in search of her doll.

Eugénie had found her. Because she would not go back to bed, Eugénie had dressed her and given her some breakfast.

Then, because she had the household to supervise, she had told Rose-Marie to play quietly with her toys and had left her alone.

She had no sooner gone downstairs than she found a tremendous commotion taking place.

An Overseer had insisted on seeing *Madame* Boisset to report that one of the game-cocks was missing.

Melita interrupted Eugénie at this point to ask:

'What are game-cocks?'

'They are the birds *Madame* keeps especially for cock-fighting,' Eugénie explained.

'*Madame* keeps fighting-cocks?' Melita asked incredulously.

She was well aware that cock-fighting was the national sport of Martinique.

She had learnt that fights were held from November to June throughout the countryside in specially prepared 'pits'.

They created great excitement and involved high betting.

The ship's officer who had told her about it

151

on the voyage from England had said:

'The fighting-cocks are coddled by their owners, carefully fed, and it is always believed they are given drugs which are kept a secret.'

He smiled as he added:

'No-one can prove this; but certainly their spurs are sharpened and their feathers trimmed, and they look very ferocious before the start of a fight.'

Melita had made up her mind there and then that one thing she had no wish to see or hear about in Martinique was cock-fighting! She could not understand a cultured Frenchwoman like *Madame* Boisset wishing to take part in a sport which was so abominably cruel.

She knew of course at once what had happened to *Madame's* precious cock.

The Overseer, according to Eugénie, had also said that during the night he had heard the Voodoo drum, but had been too frightened to investigate; but now that the cock was missing he was certain that a Voodoo ceremony had taken place in the forest.

It was then, Melita learnt, that *Madame* Boisset had flown into a temper.

She ordered that Léonore, who was the known *Mambo* of the slaves, be whipped.

Melita gasped when she heard this, for her father had explained to her how cruel and bar-

152

baric the whipping of slaves was.

It had a ritual all its own. The slave, stripped naked, was spread-eagled and tied at the wrists and ankles by leather thongs to a heavy wooden platform.

The platform was then elevated to an angle of 25 degrees, which made it easier for the man using the whip to flog his victim.

'It is always done in public,' Sir Edward had said, 'because then it is not only a punishment for the wrong-doer but also a deterrent for others!'

The idea of whipping a woman as old as Léonore filled Melita with horror.

'She have twenty lashes,' Eugénie said. 'She die!'

'How can such a thing be permitted?' Melita said almost beneath her breath.

'That not all, *M'msell.*'

'More? What worse can have happened?' Melita asked getting out of bed.

She ran to the washhand-stand, but as she reached it she heard Eugénie say:

'The slaves have taken *la petite M'mselle* prisoner!'

Melita stopped dead and turned round.

'What did you say?'

Eugénie repeated her words, speaking so quickly that it was hard at first to understand.

Apparently when she had left Rose-Marie alone the child had decided to find Philippe and ask him to make her another doll.

She had gone to the slave quarters and while she was there the slaves had learnt that Léonore, their *Mambo*, was to be whipped.

They had surged out of the sugar distillery and those who had been leaving in a gang for the plantations came back despite the Overseers' efforts to stop them.

Then before they could be prevented they had cut down trees and made a barricade across each entrance to the slave quarters.

It all happened so quickly, and they had acted, Eugénie said, in a frenzied manner like men posessed. The Overseers had run to find *Madame* Boisset, not knowing what action they should take.

By the time she had been alerted and had gone down onto the mound where she prayed with the slaves in the evenings, the barricades were up and the men behind them were refusing to give up Léonore.

Protected by their barricades, they were out of reach of the Overseers' whips and the only way they could be dislodged was with fire-arms.

According to Eugénie, *Madame* Boisset was about to give the order to shoot when she learnt that Rose-Marie was with them.

154

The slaves also realised that they had a most valuable hostage in their hands and they now refused to let Rose-Marie return to the house unless it was agreed that no punishment would be inflicted on Léonore.

When she finally understood what was happening Melita said quickly:

'*Monsieur le Comte* must be informed.'

'*Monsieur* leave early, *M'mselle!*'

'Then we must send for him!' Melita said. 'Is there anyone in the stables who can ride?'

'Yes, *M'mselle*, Jacques. He exercise horses when *Monsieur* not here.'

'Then tell him to ride immediately, as quickly as he can, to Bouillon Ajoupa,' Melita said. 'He will find the *Comte* there. Ask him to return as speedily as possible.'

'I do that,' Eugénie replied.

She left the room and Melita heard her running down the passage.

She finished dressing and, picking up her sunshade, walked out of the house and down the roadway which led towards the mound.

On it she could see the red dress of *Madame* Boisset, who was talking with four of the Overseers.

She was obviously still in a rage because, although Melita could not at first understand what she was saying, she could hear her high-

155

pitched voice rising higher with every word she spoke.

In the centre of the mound was a white pillar on which there was a cross.

Melita could not help wondering if *Madame* Boisset, who was so fond of preaching to the slaves, had ever read them the story of how Christ had been whipped by the Romans.

She reached the mound, but she did not climb up it. Instead she went round it and walked directly towards the rough barricade which stood in front of the slave quarters.

She had nearly reached it when *Madame* Boisset became aware of her.

'Where are you going, *Mademoiselle?*' she asked.

Melita did not answer and *Madame* Boisset screamed:

'*Mademoiselle*—I spoke to you! Come here immediately!'

Melita had, however, reached the barricade and she could see dark eyes peeping at her from between the trunks of the trees.

The men were crouching down, but as she stood there one rose and she recognised him as an older man whom she had seen in the sugar distillery.

'Go 'way, *M'mselle*,' he said. 'You not come here.'

156

'If *la petite M'mselle* is your prisoner,' Melita answered, 'or perhaps I should say your hostage, then as I must be with her, I am also your hostage.'

The man stared at her in astonishment. Now she realised she had also seen him the night before, sitting with closed eyes beside Philippe in the forest.

'Let me in,' Melita said.

Then in a low voice that was impossible for anyone else to hear she said:

'I have sent someone to fetch *Monsieur le Comte*. Do not surrender until he returns.'

There was a flash of white teeth as the man understood what she was saying.

Then he held out his hand. Taking it, Melita put one foot on the lowest of the piled tree-trunks and he helped her over the others.

As she stood for a moment on top of the barricade supported by the black man's hand she heard *Madame* Boisset yelling at her in a frenzy of anger.

'Come back, *Mademoiselle!* How dare you behave in such a manner! If you are shot as these slaves will be shot you will have only yourself to blame.'

Melita did not answer or even turn her head.

She was well aware that *Madame* Boisset would not dare risk shooting anyone while

Rose-Marie was in their midst.

She was helped onto the ground and as she reached it Rose-Marie came running towards her from Philippe's hut.

'*Mademoiselle! Mademoiselle!*'

She flung herself into Melita's arms, and as she bent down to kiss the child, Melita asked:

'You are not frightened?'

'No, I am not frightened,' Rose-Marie said proudly. 'Cousin Josephine is very angry, but it is wrong and wicked to beat poor Léonore. She is too old, is she not, *Mademoiselle?*'

'Much too old,' Melita agreed firmly.

'Come and see Philippe,' Rose-Marie begged. 'He is making another doll, a very pretty one.'

Melita wondered what had happened to the doll in the red dress that had been used in the Voodoo ceremony last night. Then she told herself that her most important duty at the moment was to keep Rose-Marie happy and unafraid.

She was certain that violence was out of the question, and as if in answer to her thoughts she heard one of the Overseers shout, obviously at *Madame* Boisset's instigation:

'You will be given no food or water until you behave yourselves. When you are hungry you will come out like cowed dogs. Then we will

158

see who is master.'

She felt Rose-Marie's hand tighten in hers.

'Shall we be very hungry, *Mademoiselle?*'

'Not for very long,' Melita said soothingly. 'Your Papa will be here soon, and I know he will think it wrong to hurt Léonore.'

'Cousin Josephine is very angry,' Rose-Marie said, 'and she will be angry with Papa if he interferes.'

'He will know exactly what to do,' Melita said confidently.

She knew the slaves would be waiting for his return as eagerly as she was.

Philippe was sitting in the doorway of his hut with a bundle of leaves beside him and behind him inside the desolate empty building was Léonore.

Melita stepped over the threshold.

'Everything will be all right, Léonore,' she said. 'When *Monsieur le Comte* hears what has happened he will come back, and I know he will not allow you to be punished.'

Léonore looked at Melita with her penetrating black eyes which still seemed young despite the lines of age on her face.

After a moment she said quietly:

'You saw!'

Melita made no pretence of not understanding what she meant.

159

'Yes, I saw,' she answered. 'The drum called me and I followed the sound.'

There was silence. Then Léonore said:

'You find happiness.'

She turned away as she spoke, as if she had nothing more to say.

Melita stared after her wondering how it was possible for the old woman to know so much. Yet she did not doubt for a moment that she knew she had been present at the ritual last night and that she knew also what she and the *Comte* felt for each other.

It would have somehow been wrong to ask questions.

Melita sat down beside Rose-Marie while Philippe carved away at the coconut which was to be the body of her doll.

She told them both stories that she had known and loved as a child, the story of Cinderella, and of Hansel and Gretel. Every time she finished a tale Rose-Marie clapped her hands and asked for more.

The two children seemed utterly absorbed in her story-telling.

Only Melita was vividly aware of the slaves crouching behind the barricades, of *Madame* Boisset and the Overseers watching them from the mound.

It grew very hot, and now Melita began to

understand what it would be like if they had to go without water for long.

It had to be brought from the gully which ran beneath the water-wheel.

One by one the male slaves came back from the barricades to go into the houses and drink the last dregs of what was left in the huge stone jars which their wives had carried home on their heads the night before.

'I wonder when they last ate,' she said, speaking her thoughts aloud, forgetting for the moment that Philippe was dumb.

It was Léonore who answered her and at the sound of her voice Melita started because she had thought the old woman was in the shadows at the far end of the hut instead of behind her.

'We eat at noon and when work over,' Léonore said.

'Then nobody will be very hungry as yet.'

'Always hungry,' Léonore answered. '*Madame* give too little food. Enough working men only.'

Melita's lips tightened.

It seemed incredible that *Madame* Boisset, with Cécile's large fortune to draw on, should deliberately cut the food which was given to the slaves and their families.

'But it is what I might have expected,' she thought.

161

The small children whom she had seen on her first visit to the slave quarters playing about on the grass had all been kept in their huts by their mothers in case they should be hurt by what was happening.

But now they began to emerge one after another into the sunshine, and looking at them Melita realised they were in most cases too thin for their age and height.

If she had disliked *Madame* Boisset before, she hated her now.

'Nothing could be so cruel,' she thought, 'as deliberately to deprive small children of food, especially when there is absolutely no necessity for it.'

Although Léonore said nothing, Melita had the feeling that the old woman could read her thoughts and knew what was going on in her mind.

After some minutes Melita asked:

'What do you eat?'

'Salt fish.'

'Not fish from the sea?'

'No. Salt fish come from America.'

Melita was sure it was cheaper than fresh fish although these could be caught locally.

'*Monsieur* give us crab, stew with pork, coconut and hot peppers—but no more!'

Melita heard the hunger and the greed in

the old voice.

Then because she did not wish to upset Rose-Marie in any way she continued with her story-telling, reciting nursery-rhymes, looking back into her own childhood to recall tales and jingles that had entertained her when she was the same age.

It was about half an hour after noon when Rose-Marie, pushing back her hair from her forehead, said plaintively:

'I am thirsty *Mademoiselle,* I want a drink.'

Melita thought she could have echoed the same words.

The slave quarters were surrounded by trees and if there was any breeze coming from the sea it did not reach them.

Her lips were dry and she was finding it increasingly difficult to go on talking.

'Your Papa will be here soon, dearest,' she said consolingly.

At that moment her heart leapt in her breast as she saw a cloud of dust in the distance!

Then she saw, riding up the drive at a tremendous pace, a horse and its rider.

The *Comte* rode straight up to the mound and pulled his mount to a standstill.

Madame Boisset had been away for about an hour and she had in fact just returned.

While Melita had said nothing to the children

163

she had seen, even though she was some distance away, that *Madame* Boisset held something in her hand, and she suspected that it was a pistol.

'What is going on here?' the *Comte* asked in a voice that could be heard not only by *Madame* Boisset but also by the slaves behind the barricade.

'So you have returned, Étienne,' *Madame* Boisset replied coldly. 'Perhaps you will be able to exert your authority to extricate your daughter from the hands of these criminals who are holding her prisoner.'

'Why should they be doing that?' the *Comte* enquired.

'Because we have a rebellion on our hands,' *Madame* Boisset replied, 'and make no mistake, the rebels will be punished, and punished severely, while the ring-leaders will be executed. I shall make sure of that!'

She was speaking, Melita realised, for effect and to intimidate the listening slaves.

'If this is a rebellion, which I very much doubt,' the *Comte* said, 'I would like to know the reason why it is taking place.'

He dismounted from his horse, signalled to one of the Overseers to take its bridle, and walked towards the barricade.

As he reached it the man who had assisted

164

Melita rose as he had done before to his feet.

'What is the trouble, Frédérick?' the *Comte* asked.

'We not let Léonore be whipped, *Monsieur*. She too old. Her our *Mambo*.'

'But of course she is too old,' the *Comte* replied, 'and let me make this quite clear, I will not permit any whipping on my Estate as long as it belongs to me.'

For a moment it seemed as if the slaves did not understand what they had heard, then a cheer went up and they all started to their feet.

'Will you let me through?' the *Comte* asked. 'I wish to speak to my daughter.'

Willing hands bent down to move the barricades of tree-trunks and in a moment the opening was there.

Rose-Marie jumped up from Melita's side to run towards the *Comte*.

'Papa! Papa!' she cried flinging her arms round him. 'You have been a very long time and I am thirsty. I want a drink.'

'Then we must find you one,' the *Comte* said quietly.

He looked over her head at Melita and their eyes met. Without words he told her how right she had been to send for him and how grateful he was.

165

She moved to his side.

'The slaves are hungry as well as thirsty,' she said in a low voice. 'They are not getting enough to eat. If you look at the children you will see how thin they are.'

There was an unmistakable expression of anger on the *Comte's* face.

Without speaking, but carrying Rose-Marie in his arms, he walked towards the Overseers who were standing waiting for him at the bottom of the mound.

Madame Boisset had disappeared.

'Issue treble rations to everyone,' he said, 'and there will be no work until they have eaten. Is that understood?'

'Yes, *Monsieur.*'

The Overseers were looking uncomfortable and found it difficult to meet his eyes.

'You heard what I said,' the *Comte* went on in a stern voice. 'There will be no whipping on this Estate in the future.'

'Yes, *Monsieur.*'

He turned back towards the slaves who were clearing away the barricade.

'Leave that until you have received your food,' he said, 'it is waiting for you now in the store-house. And send the women for water. You all need a drink.'

They cheered him again. Then he waited

166

until Melita was beside him, and still carrying Rose-Marie, they walked up the incline towards the house.

'I came the moment I heard what had happened,' the *Comte* said. 'I did not expect to find you in the slave quarters, but I might have guessed that you would be with Rose-Marie.'

There was a caressing note in his voice which made her feel as if she vibrated to music.

'*Mademoiselle* told us exciting stories, Papa,' Rose-Marie told him. 'Philippe enjoyed them too, although he could not say so.'

As if she suddenly remembered why she had been there she said:

'Cousin Josephine took away my doll which Philippe made for me. You must tell her Papa, that he may make me another. I like the dolls Philippe makes.'

'I will tell her,' the *Comte* said, and his tone was grim.

But he was not to speak to *Madame* Boisset that afternoon.

As they ate their luncheon, which was waiting for them when they got back to the house, there were only three of them in the Dining-Room.

Madame Boisset, they learnt, had retired to her own room.

As they finished and Eugénie came to collect Rose-Marie for her siesta, the *Comte* said to Melita:

'I cannot wait until tomorrow. I will leave for St. Pierre now. The sooner this intolerable situation is ended the better.'

'You are right,' Melita replied.

She felt she could not bear to listen to another stormy scene between *Madame* Boisset and the man she loved.

'I will come back as quickly as I can, you know that.'

'I feel sure you will be successful,' Melita answered, 'and however little you can borrow, we will somehow make it do.'

He smiled at her and there was no reason for him to say in words how much he loved her.

They stood looking at each other, until as if it was hard for him to do so the *Comte* turned away. Picking up his tall hat and his gloves, he walked across the verandah and in the direction of the stables.

Melita went upstairs to her bed-room.

Today she had no reason to go out into the garden or to look for the trees of the *Pomme d'Amour*.

There was love in her heart, love in every thought she had, in every breath she breathed. Love for a man had changed her whole world for her from the first moment they met.

'I love him!'

Her whole being seemed to move to a melody of the winds, and the music of them sang in her ears.

When Rose-Marie awoke, having slept longer because she was so tired after the excitement of the morning, Melita played to her on the piano. Then they took a walk in the garden to see the parrots and to feed the monkey.

Rose-Marie had many questions to ask, and Melita had no intention today of giving her any formal lessons.

Only as they were coming back to the house did the child say:

'I wonder in what secret place Cousin Josephine hid my doll? Shall we try to find her?'

'Not today, dearest,' Melita answered. 'Let us wait until your Papa returns, then we will ask him to tell Cousin Josephine that you may have another doll. There will then be no need to be secretive about it.'

'That will give Philippe time to make me a very, very special one, will it not?' Rose-Marie answered.

'A very special one,' Melita agreed.

Rose-Marie had her supper, then seemed quite content to go to bed.

169

She kissed Melita good-night very affectionately and asked:

'Do you know lots and lots more stories, *Mademoiselle?*'

'Lots more,' Melita replied.

'And you will tell them all to me?'

'Not all at once, and perhaps you will learn to read some of them for yourself,' Melita smiled.

'I would like that,' Rose-Marie replied. 'I do love having you here, *Mademoiselle.*'

'And I love being here,' Melita answered truthfully.

★ ★ ★ ★

When she had changed for dinner, Melita felt nervous of going downstairs to the Salon.

She had learnt from Eugénie that *Madame* was expecting her to dine with her and she was sure it was going to be a very uncomfortable meal, but she could hardly refuse.

She walked downstairs feeling that every foot-step was an effort and her feet grew heavier and heavier as she neared the Salon.

To her astonishment *Madame* Boisset, who was standing by one of the windows, turned to face her with a smile on her lips.

'Good evening, *Mademoiselle,*' she said in

170

quite a pleasant tone. 'I felt that as we are to be alone tonight we might indulge ourselves. I have poured you out a glass of madeira. I do hope you will join me.'

If Melita was surprised at the pleasantness in *Madame* Boisset's tone she was even more surprised when she saw that standing on the satin-wood table in front of the sofa there was a glass of madeira.

Another, which she knew was intended for her, was set in front of a hard upright chair on which she had sat the previous evening.

She did not like madeira, but it was impossible to say so.

Madame Boisset was just about to seat herself on the sofa when Eugénie came into the room.

'Dinner is ser—' she began.

Then with a little scream she pointed to the far corner of the Salon.

'A snake, *Madame!* A snake!'

Madame Boisset turned quickly.

'Where? Where?' she asked. 'Frighten it away, Eugénie!'

She was looking into the corner where Eugénie had pointed.

Then, to Melita's astonishment, as the maid passed the satin-wood table she exchanged the two glasses of madeira!

It was done so swiftly that Melita could

hardly realise a second later that *Madame's* glass now stood in front of her and hers was in front of the seat that *Madame* would occupy.

'I cannot see a snake!' *Madame* was saying.

'It there, *Madame*. I see it,' Eugénie insisted, 'but no worry. Men kill in morning.'

'They make me shudder!' *Madame* Boisset exclaimed.

She turned round to seat herself on the sofa.

'I expect, *Mademoiselle*, you have been told that in Martinique we have some very poisonous snakes, especially the *Fer-de-Lance*, which is deadly.'

'Dinner is served, *Madame*,' Eugénie interrupted.

'Then we must not spoil the first course by letting it get cold,' *Madame* said. 'Drink your madeira, *Mademoiselle*, and we will go into the Salon.'

She finished the glass in front of her as she spoke and Melita forced herself to drink hers before she followed in the wake of *Madame's* rustling gown.

While they were having dinner she found it difficult to believe that *Madame* was the same person who had been so rude and disagreeable to her ever since her arrival.

Now she spoke conversationally of the island, of Melita's father and his distinguished career.

172

She talked about the Empress Josephine and described to Melita her home at Trois Ilets.

'My aunt knew the family well,' *Madame* said, 'and Josephine, I understand, always had a reputation even when she was a girl for being somewhat fast and flirtatious.'

'She certainly had a very distinguished career,' Melita remarked.

'Napoleon, for all his great success in battle, was only a Corsican,' *Madame* replied.

There was the scorn in her voice of the blue-blooded Frenchwoman for what she always considered as those "inferior Corsicans".

Melita thought her father would have been amused at the snobbery of it.

'Josephine, when she was ten, was told by a fortune-teller who was descended from the Carib Indians that she would be Queen of France,' *Madame* remarked.

'Do you believe in fortune-telling, *Madame?*' Melita enquired.

'Sometimes,' *Madame* replied reflectively, 'but many of them are just liars and charlatans.'

'But where the Empress Josephine was concerned they predicted the truth.'

'A fortune-teller once told me...' *Madame* began, then stopped.

Melita waited.

173

'It is of no consequence,' *Madame* said after a long pause. 'It has not come true—yet!'

Melita thought she could guess what *Madame* had wished to know, but she dared not ask any more questions.

The dinner, which was far less elaborate than when the *Comte* was present, was soon finished and when they reached the Salon Melita curtsied.

'Thank you, *Madame. Bonsoir.*'

'Good-night, *Mademoiselle*, we have had a very pleasant talk.'

'Very pleasant, *Madame,*' Melita answered, but she was puzzled as she went upstairs.

Why had *Madame* changed?

It was impossible to believe that she had been pleased with her behaviour today when she had defied her orders and deliberately joined Rose-Marie in the slave quarters.

It was also impossible for her not to have been infuriated by the manner in which the *Comte* had conceded victory to the slaves and had in fact rewarded them with extra rations and a promise of a future free from punishment.

It was contrary, Melita thought as she went up the stairs, to everything in *Madame's* character to accept such a humiliation.

She could not help feeling, although she told

174

herself it was absurd, that it was somehow sinister.

It was obvious that *Madame* had wanted her dismissed and sent back to England. If anything could have provided an excuse for her to do so, it would have been the disobeying of her orders.

And yet, *Madame* Boisset had been charming.

'It is extraordinary! It is too difficult for me to understand,' Melita told herself.

She longed for the *Comte's* return so that she could tell him what had occurred and ask him for an explanation.

She knew that by now he would have reached St. Pierre and perhaps would have had an opportunity of going to the Bank. The idea made her pray as she had prayed while she was dressing for dinner that he would be successful.

Surely, as he and his family were so well known, the Bank would trust him?

It would be a mistake, however, to borrow too large a sum. That might prove to be a millstone round their necks.

They would have to manage with a little, and although she knew nothing about crops she could not help feeling sure that those she had seen when the *Comte* had driven her to

175

Vesonne-des-Arbres had looked healthy and plentiful.

With that money alone perhaps they could get through the winter, but of one thing she was certain, that however poor they were they would never deprive the slaves of proper nourishment.

Melita, having reached the top of the stairs, went first to the School-Room to put away the toys and to tidy the music sheets on the piano.

She peeped into Rose-Marie's bed-room and saw that she was fast asleep.

Melita bent over her to cover her bare arm with the sheet she had thrown off because it was hot when she first went to bed.

Now it was cooler, so she covered her also with a fine blanket.

When she had finished she looked down at the sleeping child, then up at the portrait of her mother which stood over the bed.

She knew the faces of the two had a similarity about them which was inescapable.

The voice she had heard coming from Léonore's lips last night might have been Rose-Marie's!

Because the idea posed a dozen questions to which she had no answers, Melita turned away and went quickly to her own bed-room.

She lit the candles beside her bed and when

176

she had done so she turned and was startled by what she saw! On a table at the other end of the room there was a doll!

It was one of Philippe's, decorated with leaves, and she thought he must have had it put there for her to give to Rose-Marie. Then as she moved it there seemed something familiar about the gown.

Startled, she suddenly realised that she had just been looking at the portrait of the person the doll depicted.

It was Cécile, there was no doubt about that!

There was a white leaf for the face and brown curls on either side to denote the hair.

The off-the-shoulder gown with its wide bertha was exactly the same as the artist had painted in the portrait over Rose-Marie's bed.

The full skirts of her gown were fashioned of the white leaves which came from one particular plant and were almost a replica of the shot muslin Cécile had worn.

Melita stood looking at the doll and felt she did not understand.

Why had Philippe made a model for her of Cécile?

She was sure that the idea had not come from the dumb and crippled boy, but from his grandmother, from Léonore, the *Mambo* from whom, Melita thought uncomfortably, nothing could be hidden.

Why? Why?

As she stood staring at the doll the question kept repeating itself over and over again in her mind.

Philippe's artistry was unmistakable.

The doll was exquisitely made and it was hard to think that in a week or so the leaves would fade and such a clever creation would wither away.

Melita stood looking at the image which Philippe had created for a long time, then when she could find no solution to the question in her mind she slowly undressed.

She had meant to read as she had come up to bed so early, but now she felt tired—tired after having slept so little the night before, tired with the emotions and anxieties of the day.

Tired with the surprises that had followed one after the other, culminating in *Madame* Boisset's strange behaviour this evening.

It was hard to think any more and wearily Melita got into bed and turned to blow out the candles.

She was vividly conscious as she did so of the doll on the other side of the room. Then deliberately she looked away from it and cuddled down against her pillow in the darkness...

She awoke suddenly with a feeling that someone had called her.

Instantly her thoughts flew to Rose-Marie.

She listened, remembering as she did so how the night before she had listened to the almost imperceptible beat of the drum.

Then, clearly and distinctly, although she was not certain whether it was that she heard it in her mind or in her ears, she heard someone say:

'Look behind the picture—look behind the picture!'

It was Cécile's voice that spoke—the voice she had heard in the forest, coming from Léonore's lips.

Melita sat up knowing her heart was pounding and she felt as if the throb of it was almost audible in the silence of the room.

'Look behind the picture!'

She had heard the words distinctly. They had been spoken—but by whom?

She had a feeling that she must act immediately. It was the same feeling that had called her from the house the night before—out into the forest.

Almost automatically she got out of bed.

The shadows were dark in the room and through the uncurtained windows there was enough light coming from the sky for her to see the outline of the furniture.

She opened the door, moved along the passage and into Rose-Marie's room.

There was the fragrance of flowers which Melita had not noticed before and as she went towards the bed Rose-Marie stirred and spoke drowsily as if she was still asleep.

'Mama!' she said. 'Mama!'

Melita stood very still.

The child's eyes were closed and she did not speak to her. Then Melita's eyes went up to the picture.

Was it her imagination, or did Cécile's figure seem for the moment to be almost luminous? She felt too as if there was someone in the room. Someone she could not see.

Then, as if she was compelled to do what she had been told to do, she put her hand on the bottom of the picture and lifted it away from the wall.

Nothing happened and she put her other hand against the back of the picture. She felt something stuck into the side of the frame.

She pulled gently and it came away in her fingers. She let the picture fall back into place.

In the darkness of the bed-room she could just discern that she held a piece of paper and an envelope.

This, she thought, was what she had been meant to find.

180

Rose-Marie did not move as she went from the room back to her own bed-chamber.

She lit the candles by her bed, then looked down at what she had found behind the picture.

There was a piece of paper just folded in two and a sealed envelope on which was written: "*Étienne*".

Melita felt a strange excitement rising within her as she unfolded the paper and bent towards the candle.

The writing was rounded but little-formed, almost the writing of a child, and was easy to read.

May 3rd, 1839

I, Cécile Marie Louise, Comtesse de Vesonne declare this to be my last and real will.

I leave everything I possess to my beloved husband, Étienne, Comte de Vesonne.

Cécile Vesonne.

Below the signature was written: '*Eugénie—this is her mark. Jeanne—this is her mark,*' and there was a roughly executed cross by each of the names.

Melita stared at what she had read, then she shut her eyes.

Her prayers had been answered and Étienne was saved as Cécile had wished him to be!

CHAPTER SIX

Melita dressed herself, putting on a thin riding-habit.

She did not light the candles; she merely felt her way round the room.

By the time she was nearly ready the sky had lightened and the stars had disappeared.

Very soon it would be dawn.

She moved on tip toe along the passage to Eugénie's room.

The maid slept only a little way from Rose-Marie so that she could hear the child if she awoke in the night and needed her.

Melita was too frightened to knock on the door in case the sound of it should disturb *Madame* Boisset who would discover what she was about to do.

Instead she turned the handle very gently. By the faint light coming from the door she could see Eugénie sleeping in a narrow wooden bed-stead.

She touched her shoulder and the maid awoke immediately.

'Do not make a noise,' Melita murmured.

'I need your help, Eugénie.'

The maid got out of bed, took a shawl from a chair and pulled it round her shoulders to cover her cotton nightgown.

'Listen,' Melita whispered, 'I have to go to St. Pierre immediately to find the *Comte*. It is very important! And I need a horse.'

'I take you stables, *M'mselle*,' Eugénie said. 'Wait downstairs, I not long.'

Melita turned towards the door and as she reached it Eugénie said in a little louder tone:

'We not wake *Madame*. She sleep heavy.'

Melita asked no question, but a few minutes later, when Eugénie joined her downstairs dressed in her usual cotton gown with a white apron she explained:

'*Madame* called me one o'clock. Bad pain! I give her sleeping herbs. She sleep long time.'

That was a relief, Melita thought, and she said as they walked quickly towards the stables:

'You will look after Rose-Marie, Eugénie? I shall be back as soon as I can.'

'No hurry,' the maid answered. '*Madame* not know you gone.'

Melita doubted this, but she was concerned with getting away before everyone was up.

Jacques was awakened by Eugénie and he put a side-saddle on a spirited chestnut horse which at any other time Melita would have been excited at the thought of riding.

Now she had only one object in mind, one goal, one desire, and that was to find the *Comte* and show him what had been hidden behind the picture of Cécile.

Jacques helped her into the saddle and she arranged the full skirt of her riding-habit over the pummel, then, turning the horse's nose west, she set off in the direction of St. Pierre.

Fortunately she was already aware that there was only one road leading to the town and it would be difficult for her to lose her way.

At the same time she was a little apprehensive about riding alone through the rain forest.

In fact she need not have been afraid because before Vesonne was out of sight dawn had come and the sunshine seemed not only to sweep away the shadows of the night but also her own fears.

Now everything was enveloped with an aura of gold, although Melita was not certain whether it was due to the happiness she felt in her heart or the sun shining on the flowers and exotic vegetation.

At first her mount was frisky, but he settled down to move at an even but swift pace and Melita was certain she would be able to reach St. Pierre in two-and-a-half hours.

Actually it took her a little longer, and when

she came down the hill with its high, shady trees into the town itself she realised that she had forgotten how large it was and how many streets there appeared to be in which she might lose her way.

She stopped the first elderly man she saw and asked if he could tell her the right direction to Château Vesonne.

She knew that this was the name of the house where Étienne's father and mother had lived after they left Vesonne-des-Arbres.

But she had no idea of the road in which it was situated or even its general location and she was half-afraid that she might have to ask innumerable times before she finally found it.

But the *Comte* was better known than she expected, for the old man pointed his finger to the left and said in a deep, guttural tone:

'Pass the Cathedral, *Madame*. Big house— you not miss.'

The Cathedral with its white turrets which Melita had seen when the ship was coming into port was an inescapable land-mark as it towered high above the red roofs of the houses around it, and was, she found, extremely impressive near-to.

Although it was so early in the morning the streets already were crowded, the women in their colourful red, orange and blue dresses

185

carrying baskets of fruit on their heads.

The men were moving loaded wicker baskets and wearing wide-brimmed basket-work hats which Melita knew were made from Caribbean straw.

There were donkeys laden with huge loads and horses dragging wooden carts loaded with freshly cut sugar cane or pineapples.

Past the Cathedral there was less traffic owing to the fact that the houses on either side of the road were large and more luxurious.

Each stood in its own garden brilliant with flowers, and as each one seemed more impressive than the last Melita began to wonder which belonged to the *Comte*.

Then a little higher up the road, standing alone in a commanding position, was a house which appeared to be different from any of the others.

Its garden was brilliant with bougainvillaea and a number of tall cypress trees stood like green sentinels at the entrance.

The house itself was built in the design of a French Château except that, like all the other Villas in the town, it had a shady verandah.

Painted grey, with grey shutters, Melita was sure it had reminded Étienne's father when he built it of his own country far away across the ocean.

There was no need to ask anyone if this was the place she was seeking. She was sure it was the *Comte's* home and as she reached the entrance and passed through a pair of wrought iron gates she saw over the top of them picked out in gold the Vesonne coat-of-arms.

There was a narrow drive, then a front door reached by a flight of steps.

Now she had arrived at her destination Melita was no longer in a hurry. At the same time she was not quite certain what she should do.

She sat a little helplessly on her horse, wondering if she should dismount and ring the bell at the side of the door.

Then a man appeared around the side of the Château and she recognised him as the groom who had travelled with the *Comte* in his chaise.

He looked at her in astonishment, then came quickly to her side.

'*Bonjour, M'mselle,*' he smiled.

'*Bonjour,*' Melita replied.

Now she had seen a friendly face she somehow felt surer of herself.

She dismounted and walked to the door, but before she reached it an elderly man appeared.

He had grey hair and wore the white linen coat of a servant.

'Is *Monsieur le Comte* at home?' Melita asked.

There was a little tremor in her voice as for the first time she wondered what she would do if by any chance Étienne had already left the house. It might be hard to find him in such a big town.

'*Monsieur* is having breakfast, *M'mselle.*'

Melita stepped into the hall. As was usual in hot countries the doors were all open and through the Salon she could see the man she was seeking sitting on the verandah outside.

The *Comte* was reading the newspaper, until as if she called to him without words he turned his head and saw her.

She ran towards him, crossing the hall, passing through the Salon; and by the time he had taken only two steps in her direction she had reached him.

'Melita, my darling, what are you doing here?' he asked in astonishment.

'Oh, Étienne, I have something for you, something which is so wonderful that I can hardly believe it is true.'

'You have ridden all this way alone?' he asked in a tone of consternation.

'Yes...yes,' Melita said impatiently, 'but it was not difficult. I had to see you and I dared not wait.'

She undid the buttons of her riding-jacket as she spoke and drew from her breast where she had kept them safe the piece of paper and the envelope she had found behind the picture in Rose-Marie's bed-room.

She held them out to the *Comte* who took them automatically but his eyes were on her face.

'I can hardly believe you are here,' he said. 'I was thinking about you all night, longing for you.'

'Read what I have brought you,' Melita said insistently. 'Read them!'

He smiled at her impatience, then unfolded the piece of paper on which Cécile had written her will.

He stared at it, and having read it through, read it again.

'You found this?' he asked after what seemed to Melita to be a long silence.

She had been watching him.

There was a little pause before she answered:

'Yes...I found it. I will tell you how in a moment. Is it...is it valid?'

She expressed the fear which had lain at the back of her mind all the time she had been riding to St. Pierre.

Supposing legally the will was unacceptable? Then it would have raised her hopes and the *Comte's* unnecessarily.

He looked again at the date.

'This will was executed two days after the other,' he said after a moment.

'That is what I hoped,' Melita said.

As if the relief was almost too much for her she sat down in the nearest chair which stood at the breakfast table.

The *Comte* put Cécile's will down on the table and stared at the envelope.

'You have not read this?'

'No, it was addressed to you.'

He took a silver knife from the table, slit it open and drew out the piece of paper which was inside.

He read it slowly and Melita watched him as she had done before.

Then with an expression on his face which she did not understand and in complete silence he handed it to her.

As she took it he walked away to stand on the edge of the verandah, holding on to one of the iron posts which supported it and staring blindly into the sunlit garden.

Fearfully Melita looked down at what he had given her and read:

My Dearest Husband:
Josephine has made me Sign a wicked Will in which I Leave her all my Money. I knew it was Wrong of Me, but I could not help Myself. I am

190

sorry, so very sorry, but I have written Another which I will hide so that She cannot find it.

Forgive me.

I am your devoted wife,
Cécile.

The writing was clear, but beneath it written in an entirely different manner with dozens of blots there was scrawled:

I think Josephine is trying to Kill me. She gave Me a glass of Madeira to drink. It made Me very sick and during the Night I had bad pains.

Today she asked Me to have another glass and when I refused She brought Me coffee and it tasted very strange. She forced Me to drink some and I am afraid—very afraid because I am sure She means Me to die! Save Me, Étienne! Only You can save Me, and if You do not come Home soon it will be too la...

The writing squiggled away into nothing and now there was a great blot as if the pen had fallen on the paper.

Melita raised her eyes.

Now she knew why *Madame* Boisset had been so pleasant yesterday evening and why she had offered her a glass of madeira.

But Eugénie had changed the glasses and it

191

was *Madame* Boisset who had been ill in the night.

It seemed inconceivable, and yet she knew that she had escaped being murdered by a hair's breadth.

'Étienne,' she began almost in a whisper, 'there is something I must tell you.'

But as she looked at him she realised that he was suffering. He could not bear to think of his child-like wife being murdered because Josephine Boisset desired him for herself.

It was then Melita knew that what she had to tell him would alleviate some of his suffering.

It was Cécile who had come back from the grave to save him from the evil machinations of her cousin.

Cécile who had spoken through the lips of Léonore, Cécile who had awakened her to tell her where the will was hidden.

For a moment Melita felt very young and too inexperienced to cope with such a situation.

Then she knew that all that mattered was that she should comfort and sustain the *Comte* because she loved him.

She pulled her riding-hat from her head, and going to his side she slipped her hand into his.

'I have something to tell you,' she said gently. 'Shall we go into the garden? I feel it would be easier to talk to you among the flowers and in the shade of the trees.'

He did not answer. He merely drew her by the hand as if she was a child across the garden lawn to where, shaded by palms and surrounded by shrubs, there was a balustrade of white marble.

From it there was an incredibly lovely view of the sea and to the right Mont Pelée was under big white clouds.

The ground fell away beneath the balustrade and when they seated themselves on a wooden seat they could not see the roofs of the town, only the blue of the sea and the misty horizon.

Melita did not relinquish the *Comte's* hand, but held it tightly in both hers.

Then, very simply, not looking at him, but with her eyes on the sea she told him everything that had happened since he had kissed her under the fruit trees.

When she told him of the Voodoo ceremony in the forest his fingers tightened, otherwise he did not move.

He did not interrupt her story, nor did he ask any questions.

Only when she told him how *Madame* Boisset had offered her a glass of madeira and how Eugénie had exchanged the glasses did she feel him stiffen beside her and draw in a deep breath of what she thought was anger.

She continued her narrative, telling him how she had found Philippe's doll in her bed-room and how she had known it was a replica of Cécile.

'I heard a voice quite...clearly as I awoke telling me to look behind the picture,' Melita said. 'It was the same...voice that I had heard in the forest;...a voice not...unlike...Rose-Marie's.'

She paused for a moment before she went on:

'When I went into Rose-Marie's bed-room she murmured: "Mama! Mama!" in her sleep and I had the feeling that...someone was...there in the...room.'

She paused, trying to recall every detail.

'The portrait over the bed seemed...luminous but then when I found what was...hidden behind the picture...she had...gone!'

There was a long silence, then the *Comte* said:

'I can hardly credit what happened, and yet you found the will and the letter.'

'I found them,' Melita said.

The *Comte* gave a deep sigh.

'I can only blame myself,' he said, 'for not insisting on sending Josephine away when I wished to do so. I felt that her influence over Cécile was wrong and oppressive.'

His voice was sad as he continued:

'But because I was working so hard I did not

194

wish her to be lonely, and she had clung to her older cousin all her life.'

'I can understand...exactly what you felt,' Melita said. 'But darling Étienne, no amount of...regretting can alter what has...happened. We have to think of the future...both for you and for...Rose-Marie.'

The *Comte* straightened his shoulders.

'You are right, as you are always right,' he said. 'It is the future that counts, not only for ourselves but also for those who have always lived at Vesonne and worked on the estate.

'I did not realise until yesterday how badly they were being treated, and the fact that they were kept short of food is something I will never forgive.'

'They only have salt fish,' Melita said.

'How angry my father would have been!' the *Comte* exclaimed. 'However poor we were, he always insisted that the slaves' diet was varied. They enjoy a modification of the dishes which are peculiarly African.'

'Léonore told me that you gave them crab and pork stew, grated coconuts and hot peppers.'

The *Comte* smiled.

'It sounds exotic, and they also like *Sansam* which is pounded poached corn, mixed with salt or sugar, but the coloured people on each of the islands of the Caribbean have special names for their dishes. In Barbados they ask for *Coucou* and *Jug-jug.*'

'They can have all those things when you return?' Melita asked.

'Thanks to you, my darling.'

'No, we must always be grateful to...Cécile... and Léonore!'

The *Comte* did not reply, but she knew that in his heart he believed they had saved him.

After a moment she said tentatively:

'The slaves in Barbados are free.'

'For eight years, since 1834.'

'Why not here?'

'Because the French are very cautious. But I do not think their freedom will be long delayed now.'

'I hope not!' Melita exclaimed.

'The planters were convinced that to set free their work force,' the *Comte* said, 'would mean financial disaster. However, in Antigua the very opposite happened!'

'You mean they made money?' Melita enquired.

'They became richer than they had ever been before.'

When they left the verandah Melita had carried with her both Cécile's will and the letter she had left for Étienne.

Now as they spoke of money she put them into his hands.

'I think you should take these at once to an Attorney and make sure that this will terminates all the evil that has emanated from the last one.'

'I will do that,' the *Comte* agreed. 'And I am certain there will be no difficulty. The Lawyer who looked after my father's estates and mine was appalled at Josephine being left all Cécile's money, but there was nothing he could do about it.'

'Did he try?' Melita asked.

'It was useless, the will had been properly witnessed and Cécile had been left by her father in a position where she could do what she wished with her own fortune.'

'Go and see him now,' Melita urged. 'I shall not feel really happy until I am sure that this will is acceptable. After all, Eugénie and Jeanne could not write their names.'

The *Comte* smiled at the anxiety in her tone.

'A mark is quite legal here in this country where so few people are able to write,' he answered, 'and I think the letter which Cécile left for me will prove quite clearly that Josephine must be deranged.'

He suddenly put his arms around Melita and drew her against him.

197

'Oh, my precious darling, suppose she had succeeded in killing you too? How could I have gone on living, knowing that I should not have left you at Vesonne alone with that fiend?'

'It was Eugénie who saved me,' Melita said. 'Perhaps she has known all the time how Cécile died. I wonder why she did not say anything?'

'I expect she thought, quite rightly, that it would be difficult, if not impossible, for me to believe her,' the *Comte* replied. 'Josephine herself would naturally have denied most forcefully such an accusation and a white person's word would always be accepted against that of a black.'

He thought for a moment before he went on:

'Eugénie must have decided that it was best to say nothing but look after Rose-Marie whom she has adored ever since she was a baby.'

'She will be safe now?' Melita asked in sudden fear.

'Eugénie would never allow anyone to hurt a hair of Rose-Marie's head!' the *Comte* said positively, 'and it will not be long before we return.'

He did not kiss Melita, he only held her very close against him.

She knew it would not have been right for them to express passionately their love for each other while he was still grieving for the child-

198

like wife who had been murdered just because he was an attractive man.

He laid his cheek for a second against her fair hair then said:

'I will go to the Attorney now, and at least I will not have to keep my appointment with the Bank this morning.'

'You have not yet asked for the loan?' Melita enquired.

'I asked, but I was told there would have to be a discussion among the senior members of the staff and they would give me my answer this morning.'

Melita knew by his tone that it had hurt his pride to have to beg for money.

Now, she thought, unless something went very wrong, he was the possessor of a huge fortune.

The *Comte* rose to his feet.

'Come, my darling,' he said. 'I will take you back to the house and while I am gone you must have a bath and rest.'

He looked down at the habit she was wearing.

'I wish I had seen you on the horse, but there will be plenty of time for that. I think you will find that my sister when she was staying here last year left some gowns in her bed-room which you could wear.'

199

He smiled.

'I remember her saying that they were too thin to take to her home in Sweden where she lives with her husband.'

When they reached the foot of the stairs the *Comte* kissed Melita's hand and as she left him she heard him calling to the groom to bring round his chaise.

It was only when she was in the bed-room that belonged to the *Comte's* sister that Melita realised that she was indeed exhausted.

It was not only the long ride, it was also the anxiety she had felt and the fear that she now knew had been very real that she would not be able to escape from Vesonne.

A young maid-servant prepared her a bath and after she had bathed and felt cool and clean she dressed herself in an attractive flowered muslin gown which had been hanging in the wardrobe.

It was too large in the waist, but Melita drew it tight with a blue sash which matched the colour of her eyes and hoped after she had arranged her hair that the *Comte* would think she looked pretty.

She had taken a long time bathing and changing, but there was no sign of him when she went downstairs to the Salon.

By now it was growing hot even on the verandah, so she sat down on a comfortable sofa and feeling it was a sensible thing to do she put up her feet and laid her head against the silk cushions.

She looked round the room. It was elegantly shaped and very French in its furnishings. But she was aware that the curtains and covers of the gilt-framed furniture were faded and the carpet almost threadbare.

'The walls need painting,' she thought. 'Decorations deteriorate so quickly in the heat!'

She gave a deep sigh.

If only Cécile's will was proved to be legal the *Comte* would have the money to do everything he wished both at Vesonne and here.

'He is so...wonderful,' she thought.

The next thing she knew was that she was being awakened by being kissed.

As she opened her eyes she found that the *Comte* was kneeling beside her and kissing her passionately and demandingly.

She felt a warm tide of wonder seep through her whole body. Then, holding her so close that she could hardly breathe, he said excitedly:

'My wonderful, marvellous darling! Everything is all right! The Lawyers say that there is no question that Cécile's last will supersedes everything she had signed previously.

Oh, lovely one, how can I thank you?'

He was kissing her again and it was difficult for Melita to think of anything but the rapturous sensation he aroused in her and the thrills which ran through her body, making her feel as if she vibrated to the sunshine.

'I love you! I love you!' the *Comte* was saying.

Then at last, as if he forced himself to do so, he released her and rose to his feet to stand looking down at her flushed cheeks, shining eyes, and lips red and warm from his kisses.

'Luncheon is ready,' he said. 'It has been waiting for over an hour, but I had so much to do.'

A little unsteadily Melita got to her feet.

She loved him so much that it was difficult to understand what he was saying.

He put out his arms and drew her to him.

'I have plans for this afternoon,' he said, 'but first you must be hungry—and I know I am!'

'The maid brought me some coffee while I was having my bath,' Melita said, 'but I admit to feeling a little hollow inside.'

'Then you will enjoy your luncheon,' he smiled, 'and that is important because we have not a great deal of time.'

'We are going back to Vesonne?' Melita asked.

'Not today,' he answered. 'We are being married!'

'Married?'

Melita stared at him wide-eyed.

'Married, my precious,' the *Comte* repeated. 'Do you think for one moment that I intend to let you out of my sight or indeed out of my arms? You have been through enough dangers already and I shall only feel safe when you are my wife.'

He saw the radiance which transformed Melita's face into a beauty that held him spellbound, then he said:

'Am I moving too fast for you, my beloved? Perhaps I should have asked you first my lovely, adorable Sweetheart. Will you marry me?'

'You know I...want to be your...wife,' Melita answered.

'I was sure of it when I interviewed the Mayor,' the *Comte* said. 'I was even more sure when I arranged that the religious service should take place in the Lady Chapel of the Cathedral.'

Melita laid her cheek against his shoulder. It was impossible to find words to tell him what she felt.

'And because I know that a wedding is very important to a woman and she wishes to look her best,' the *Comte* continued, 'one of the

203

reasons why I have been away from you for so long is that I have bought you a wedding gown!'

'A wedding gown?' Melita exclaimed.

'I hope it will fit you,' he answered, 'but first things first. Our luncheon, my precious, takes priority on this occasion.'

He drew her into the Dining-Room and they ate what Melita was sure was delicious food, but it was difficult for her to taste anything.

All she was conscious of was the *Comte's* eyes looking into hers, of knowing that every word he spoke expressed his love.

They drank a little champagne, then they went upstairs side by side, their arms around each other, to change for the wedding ceremony.

The *Comte* left her at the door of her bed-room.

'Make yourself look very beautiful, my darling,' he said, 'although I cannot believe it is possible for you to look more perfect than you do at this moment.'

Melita laughed because she was so happy.

When she went into the bed-room it was to find the young maid who had brought her her bath and the old cook who was the wife of the man-servant waiting to attend her.

They had unpacked the gown that the *Comte*

had bought in the town, and it was, Melita saw at once, very lovely.

The skirt was frill upon frill of white tulle billowing out from a tiny waist, the sleeves were also fashioned of narrow frills and the tight bodice revealed the curves of her figure.

There was a veil of the finest Brussels lace which the old cook told Melita had been in the Vesonne Family for generations, and for her head there was the conventional wreath of orange blossom, made with real flowers.

She knew that nothing she had ever worn had become her better.

She knew too that when she stared at her reflection in the mirror there was a softness and spirituality about her face that had never been there before.

'Let me look at you!' the *Comte's* voice said from the doorway and she turned to realise that if she looked attractive he was positively magnificent!

He was wearing the full traditional evening dress which Frenchmen always wore when they were married.

His white shirt and muslin cravat seemed to give him, with his long-tailed close-fitting coat, a presence and an authority that had not been there before.

He seemed somehow taller and she knew it

was because for the first time for years he was not beset with anxiety and troubled about the future.

'*M'mselle est ravissante, Monsieur!*' the old cook murmured as he moved across the room towards Melita.

'*Tout á fait ravissante!*' the *Comte* agreed and to Melita he added in a low voice:

'More beautiful that I imagined any woman could be!'

He raised her hand to his lips and she felt a thrill run through her like quicksilver. Then he drew her, the full skirts of her gown rustling behind her, down the stairs to where outside the front door his chaise was waiting.

It was open, but to protect them from the sunshine overhead there was a white canopy ornamented with a silk fringe.

The *Comte* helped Melita inside and she found on her seat a bouquet of white orchids so lovely and delicate that she gave a little cry of delight.

'They are exquisite!'

'Like you, my adorable one,' the *Comte* said softly.

The groom released the horses' heads and jumped up behind. Then they were off, driving down the narrow streets to the Town Hall.

Here they made a declaration of marriage

206

before the Mayor, resplendent with his chain of office and wearing a tricolour sash.

Then, after receiving his congratulations because by Law they were now man and wife, they drove to the Cathedral.

It was cool and dim inside the great building, candles flickered in front of the statues of the Saints and there were a dozen high candles on the altar of the Lady Chapel which was massed with flowers.

A Priest was waiting for them and because Melita was not a Catholic the Service was very short.

Yet she felt as if it was attended by a choir of angels and her heart joined with theirs in a paean of thanksgiving.

She was being married to the man she loved!

She heard the *Comte* repeat his vows very solemnly, and she knew that he dedicated himself to her as she did to him.

She hoped as she prayed that she would make him a good wife, that her father was near her and that he knew how happy she was.

Then it was impossible to think of anything but the *Comte* kneeling beside her and his ring encircling the third finger of her left hand.

They went out into the sunshine to find that quite a crowd had gathered on the steps of the Cathedral.

A marriage was always an excitement, but most people in the crowd recognised the *Comte* and they cheered him, shouting their good wishes, while the women and children pelted Melita with flower petals.

They drove back to the Château and there the servants greeted them and there was champagne waiting in the Salon.

Only when they were alone did the *Comte* glance at the clock on the mantelpiece and, putting his arms around Melita, say:

'Come, my darling.'

She looked at him in surprise, wondering where they could be going. He took her across the hall, up the stairs and along the passage until he opened the door of a room at the end of it.

They entered a very large room with three windows looking out over the garden towards the sea, but it was difficult at first to notice anything but the huge bed.

Carved in gilt it was draped with silk from a corolla in the fashion of the Royal beds at Versailles.

On the back, embroidered on Madonna-blue velvet, was the coat-of-arms of Vesonne with all its colourful quarterings.

'My father brought it with him from France,' the *Comte* explained. 'When I was a child it was at Vesonne, and we will move it back to its rightful place.'

He shut the door beside him, then walked to Melita's side to take her in his arms.

'At last,' he said. 'I can tell you how much I love you and that you are mine as you have been from the first moment I saw you. Mine completely and absolutely. My wife!'

His lips were on hers before Melita could reply and now his kisses were passionate, demanding and fiercely insistent.

There was a fire in them that had not been there before and while she quivered a little from the intensity of it she knew that he awoke a flame within her and she longed for him to go on kissing her.

She wanted him to hold her closer and closer still, but he took his lips from hers to take the wreath from her head and then the veil.

He threw them down casually on a chair, then drawing her to him again, his lips on hers, he began to undo the buttons at the back of her gown.

She looked at him questioningly and as usual he knew what she was thinking.

'We are on French soil, my darling,' he said, 'and do you know what *cinq-à-sept* means in France?'

Melita thought back into the past. Somehow

209

it was connected in her mind with what her father had told her about Paris, but for the moment she could not remember.

'We missed our siesta today,' the *Comte* said, 'and to a Frenchman in Europe five to seven in the afternoon is always the time that is set aside for love!'

'I thought it was a...time for...rest.'

'Do you think I can let you rest?' he asked.

He pulled her almost roughly back into his arms and after a moment she felt her gown slip from her shoulders and from her waist to the floor.

Her petticoats followed, then the *Comte* lifted her in his arms.

Holding her lips with his, evoking a wild, ecstatic response from her heart and her very soul, he carred Melita towards the great ancestral bed.

★ ★ ★ ★

It was much cooler and the shadows in the garden were purple on the grass when finally Melita stirred.

'Are you...awake?' she whispered.

'It would be impossible for me to sleep when I am so happy,' the *Comte* answered.

'I have made...you happy?'

210

'You know you have, my sweet darling.'

Her long fair hair lay over her shoulders and he swept it back from her face to kiss very gently first her eyes, then her forehead, then one of her small ears.

'Could anyone be more entrancing, more perfect?' he asked.

'I did not know that...love could be so... wonderful.'

'I have so much to teach you, my precious.'

He gave a little sigh.

'In fact we have so much to give each other that a thousand years would not be long enough.'

'That is what I was...thinking,' Melita said, 'and we must never...lose our...happiness.'

'That would be impossible for us,' he answered. 'As I have said before, you are a part of me and we are indivisible, joined spiritually as well as physically. Nothing shall separate us and even in death we shall be together.'

He felt Melita shiver and he said:

'Forget all that has made you afraid, at least for tonight. Tomorrow we will face anything that has to be faced courageously, with kindness and understanding. Tonight is ours!'

He kissed her lips, then he asked:

'What would you like to do on your wedding

night, *ma belle?* Would you like to visit St. Pierre or to listen to music?'

Melita looked at him in consternation, then she realised that he was teasing her.

'No...I only want to be with...you.'

'That is what I wanted you to say,' he answered, 'and I have ordered a dinner which will be ready very shortly. I want a long night ahead of us, a night that will seem far too short and pass far too swiftly because I shall be making love to you.'

Melita blushed and hid her face against his.

'You make me...shy,' she murmured.

He put his fingers under her chin and turned her face up to his.

'You are like a flower opening to the sunshine. The sunshine which is part of my love.'

She moved a little closer to him, then she asked:

'What are we going to do?'

'We are going to have dinner here,' he said. 'Not downstairs in the formality of the Dining-Room but in the *Boudoir* next door. I hope what you find there will please you.'

He kissed her again before he said:

'You will find something special to wear in the wardrobe. I bought it at the same time as I bought your wedding gown. I want to see you in it.'

'It is here...in this...room?' Melita asked.

'It is your room now, my beloved,' the *Comte* replied. 'This is the most important room in the house and who else should it belong to but *Madame la Comtesse?*'

'That does not...sound like...me,' Melita protested.

'But it is you,' he answered. 'My *Comtesse*, my wife, my woman—and my love!'

The deep note in his voice made her quiver as he said:

'I knew when I saw you standing beneath the *Pomme d'Amour* that if I could not possess you I had no wish to go on living. Now that I have, my life is fulfilled. You are everything that I dreamt of, longed for, and all my ambitions for the future in one small person.'

Melita looked up at him.

'When I left England,' she said, 'I did not know that I was sailing to happiness...to a Paradise that few people are...privileged to find in this world.'

'That is what I want you to feel,' the *Comte* said, 'that we are in a special secret Paradise together because we love each other.'

'It is...true,' Melita said, 'and nothing could be more...beautiful or more like Paradise on... earth than...Vesonne.'

Even as she spoke she thought that *Madame*

213

Boisset was like a serpent in the Garden of Eden! Then she told herself that she would not think of that evil woman, at this moment when she was so happy.

But the *Comte* was already aware of where her thoughts had taken her.

'Forget her,' he said gently. 'When we were being married in the Cathedral I thanked God not only for you and that I have been so fortunate in my life, but also because ultimately, as He directs us, good will always triumph over evil.'

'I want to be...sure of that,' Melita murmured. 'I want us...both to do what is right and...good and make...everyone around us... happy.'

'We will do that,' the *Comte* said and it was a vow.

He left Melita to go into another room and when she had washed she looked in the wardrobe.

She found there the most exquisite négligée of shaded chiffon she had ever seen and she knew he had bought it because the colours were the same as the blossom on the trees of the *Pomme d'Amour*.

The trimmings on the sleeves and round the hem of the gown were of white feathers so soft and delicate that they might have been the feathery petals of the blossom.

It was almost transparent, and although there was a nightgown to go beneath it Melita felt as though she was very inadequately clad as she moved across the room towards the door which led into the *Boudoir*.

She knew that the *Comte* was waiting for her, she had heard his deep voice speaking to the servants, and now when she opened the door she saw him and it was impossible for a few seconds to see anything but him.

'You look like love itself!' he said.

Then as she moved towards him Melita realised that the room was decorated with flowers and the whole *Boudoir* had become a bower of fragrance and beauty.

There were many flowers of which she did not know the names and there were some white orchids which she had carried in her bouquet. The vases held great bunches of blossom from the *Pomme d'Amour* trees.

And behind them there was the green of the ferns which she had admired in the rain forest.

She was holding on to the *Comte's* hands because she wanted to touch him but she managed to say as she looked at the flowers:

'You have done this for...me!'

'It is a background for your beauty,' he answered. 'As I told you before, you yourself

215

are like a flower.'

She looked at him with shining eyes and would have lifted her lips to his, but at that moment the servants came in with the food.

It was a dinner she would always remember, Melita thought, a meal at which their happiness seemed to sparkle like the wine they drank.

When they had finished they sat talking a long while until the stars came out and the moonlight touched the restless waves as they came rolling in to the shore.

It was then that Melita felt as though they were isolated on a little island of their own, 'an island of flowers', as Martinique had once been called.

Now it was an island which she knew was secret for them both and where the world could not encroach.

It was their special place, the place where they were together and where, whatever happened outside, nothing could harm the essential oneness that they had become with marriage.

Finally the *Comte* rose from the table and drew Melita to the window.

They stood looking out at the moonlight and after a moment he said:

'Today we have started a new life together, a life which I believe will bring us great happiness, my darling. There will be ups and downs, difficulties and problems—that is in-evitable—but I believe that the love I have for you and you for me will deepen and grow stronger and more intense as the years pass.'

'I am...sure of that,' Melita whispered.

'Today in Church I dedicated myself to making you happy,' the *Comte* said. 'In the past I have failed in not making people as happy as I wished them to be, but you are different.'

He kissed her hair and said solemnly:

'For you and your happiness I would storm the gates of Heaven or go down into the depths of hell. There is nothing I would not do for you!'

'I love...you!' Melita said. 'They are three such...inadequate words to describe what I...feel. You have opened up a new world to me, you have shown me new horizons that I did not even know existed.'

She turned her face against his shoulder and begged:

'Help me not to fail you, help me to give you...everything you want from a...woman.'

'Not only from a woman but from myself,' the *Comte* replied. 'We are one, Melita, and if your success is mine, then my failure will also be yours.'

He smiled as he pulled her close.

'There will be no failure! There will only be love between us, love and understanding from now until eternity.'

CHAPTER SEVEN

'It is like a miracle!' Melita exclaimed.

She was sitting at the breakfast-table looking across the garden to the sea.

'What is?' the *Comte* enquired, dropping the newspaper he had been glancing through after he had finished eating.

What, Melita thought, could be more beautiful than the garden with its brilliant flowers and the sunshine glinting on the leaves of the shady trees which were silhouetted against the vivid blue of the sky.

The fragrance of freshly ground coffee and the aroma of newly baked *croissants* mingled with the scent of the flowers, and her happiness was part of the beauty and the light around her.

She turned at the Comte's question to smile at him.

'When the ship which carried me from England came into harbour,' she replied, 'I was afraid...afraid of arriving in a country of which I knew nothing...and most of all...afraid of what my new employer would be like.'

'And now you know him...?' the *Comte* asked.

'...I find he is the most wonderful man in the whole world,' Melita replied.

She put out her hand as she spoke. He took it and kissed her fingers.

'It is a miracle for me too,' he answered, 'such an amazing, unbelievable miracle, that I can hardly believe it is true!'

Melita felt herself thrill at the deep note in his voice and as she leant instinctively towards him the sunshine flashed on the ring that she wore on her third finger.

She felt as if it dazzled her in the same way that her happiness did.

It was when she was drying herself after having a bath and regretting that she had nothing more attractive to wear than the riding-habit in which she had ridden from Vesonne to St. Pierre that the maid had come into the room with her arms full of dress-boxes.

'These have just arrived for you, *Madame.*'

'For me?' Melita queried.

When she opened the boxes she understood that once again the *Comte* had thought of her.

He had known without her having to express it in words that she would want to look beautiful for him on the first day of their marriage, and when they drove back to Vesonne-des-

Arbres as man and wife.

The gown he had chosen was of turquoise blue which she knew made her skin look dazzlingly white and accentuated the deeper blue of her eyes.

There was not only a gown in a soft material that she knew would seem cool as the day grew hotter, but there was also a fashionable satin mantle made with cape sleeves, and a bonnet trimmed with the same colour.

The soft shadowy lace inside it would frame her face.

Melita let the maid help her into the gown, then, hardly pausing to look at her reflection in the mirror, she ran impulsively into the *Comte's* room.

He was standing at his high dressing table as she entered, a pair of ivory-backed hairbrushes in his hands. He was dressed only in a soft white linen shirt and tight, hose-pipe trousers.

They made him look very broad-shouldered above his narrow hips and very masculine.

Melita stood for a moment in the doorway thinking as she had thought so often before that he was the most attractive man she had ever seen.

As he put down the brushes and turned towards her she ran to his side.

'I came to show you my new gown,' she said. 'Thank you, Étienne...thank you for...thinking of it.'

She raised her face to his, his arms went round her and he pulled her against him.

'You are pleased?'

'I am thrilled!' she answered. 'You seem to know exactly what will suit me and I want you to think I look...pretty.'

'Could I think anything else?' he asked.

His lips found hers and he kissed her passionately, pulling her closer until it was hard to breathe.

'I adore you!' he said at length in a deep voice. 'Shall I take you back to bed?'

'Étienne!'

Melita pretended to be shocked and as the colour rose in her cheeks she said almost reprovingly:

'I merely came to...show you my new... gown.'

'It becomes you,' he said, 'but I am interested in what is inside it.'

She laughed shyly, extricated herself from his arms and moved towards the door.

'Breakfast is ready.'

'I see I have for a wife a very prim and proper little *Comtesse,*' he remarked.

She made a grimace at him and would have

222

left the room, but he stopped her.

'Come here!' he ordered.

She hesitated, looking at him warily, at the same time knowing that when he kissed her she found it impossible to refuse him anything.

'Come here, Melita!' he insisted.

She moved towards him slowly, her eyes questioning his.

'I have a present for you,' he said when she reached his side.

'Another present? But you have given me so much already.'

'This is something special. I should have liked to give it to you yesterday, but it had to be altered.'

He took from the table near him a velvet jewel-box and when he opened it Melita saw that it contained a ring.

It was a very large sapphire the colour of the sea, surrounded by diamonds.

'Oh, Étienne!'

It was difficult to say more as it was in fact the most beautiful ring she had ever seen.

The *Comte* drew it from the case, then taking her hand in his he kissed her third finger, already encircled with his wedding-ring, and slipped the sapphire onto it.

'For my wife!' he said softly.

'It is beautiful!'

223

Melita flung her arms around the *Comte's* neck.

'Thank you...oh, thank you,' she cried. 'Everything you do is so...wonderful, so... perfect in every way. I love you! Oh, Étienne, how much I love you!'

He kissed her until she was breathless. Then they had gone downstairs hand in hand to where breakfast was waiting for them on the verandah.

Now as the *Comte* kissed her fingers Melita said with a little catch in her voice:

'I wish we could...stay here. I am...afraid of leaving a place where I have been so...happy.'

'We will come back, and very soon,' the *Comte* said consolingly. 'We will not only need to buy your trousseau in St. Pierre, but I have ordered a necklace to match your ring.'

'You must not give me so much,' Melita protested. 'I feel that I have nothing to give you in return.'

The *Comte* smiled.

'You have given me not only a fortune and my peace of mind,' he answered. 'You have also given me something which is much more important—yourself, my precious one.'

Her fingers tightened on his.

'I feel it is not...enough,' she answered. 'There is so much...more I want to...give you.'

224

'That is one of the reasons why we will come back here,' he said, 'where we can be alone without distractions and I can teach you, my beloved little wife, about love.'

He released her hand and stood up.

'Come,' he said. 'We have to face our problems and the sooner the better. Let me make you quite sure of one thing, Melita, I do not intend to be defrauded of a honeymoon! A honeymoon, my dearest heart, where we will be completely alone as we were last night.'

Again Melita felt her colour deepen as she recalled the wonder and ecstasy they had experienced together and the rapture she felt at his kisses and the touch of his hands.

The *Comte* drew her to her feet.

'What we have to do is not going to be easy,' he said quietly, 'but you have given me a courage I have never had before.'

They set off from the Château in the *Comte's* chaise and although the sun was bright there was a cool breeze blowing from the sea.

Melita could not help feeling depressed at leaving behind the attractive town with its red roofs.

They passed the Cathedral which she knew would always be a precious memory because of the vows they had made together in the Lady Chapel, and the Town Hall, as imposing as the

Mayor himself, in which they had been legally married according to the laws of France.

The fruit trees were bright with blossom and were moving in the wind as they drove along the sea-front, and they stopped for a few moments at a toy shop.

Then they had left the town behind and were climbing the shaded road which led towards the forests.

Every mile which took them nearer and still nearer to Vesonne made Melita feel, despite the *Comte's* presence, a little more afraid.

It was not, she told herself, that *Madame* Boisset could hurt either of them now. They were married and Cécile's will, they had been assured, was legal.

It was just that she shrank from the thought of a scene, and of enduring *Madame's* rudeness and her inevitable anger.

Besides which Melita knew only too well that the effect on Rose-Marie would be harmful.

She told herself that however many children she gave the *Comte*, and she hoped there would be many, she would always love the little girl who had lost her mother and who, until now, had lived a lonely, companionless life.

'For Rose-Marie and everyone else who lives at Vesonne there will be happiness in the future,' Melita promised herself.

The chaise drove through the gorges of the rain-forest and now they were on the higher land with its crops of sugar cane on either side of the road.

'Next year we will cultivate more land,' the *Comte* said aloud. 'There are many experiments I want to make, but which I did not have a chance to put into operation in the past.'

'That will be exciting!' Melita said, but her voice was flat because they were getting nearer to Vesonne.

The *Comte* took one hand from the reins to put it over hers.

'I will look after you, my precious,' he said, 'and after this we will create an entirely different atmosphere at Vesonne. It will be what it was like when I was a boy. I thought it the most perfect place that could possibly exist this side of Heaven.'

'Anywhere would be Heaven with...you,' Melita replied, 'but especially Vesonne because it is so beautiful.'

The *Comte* turned to smile at her and she knew as his eyes rested on her face that he thought her beautiful too.

'I am so happy, so blessed,' Melita told herself. 'Please, God, do not let *Madame* Boisset say anything to spoil our happiness!'

It was a prayer she repeated as the horses

227

drove over the bridge and proceeded up the drive of Vesonne until they were within sight of the store-houses and the water-wheel.

As they neared them, as if at a signal, the slaves came pouring out of the sugar distillery and running from their huts towards them.

Melita felt the *Comte* stiffen although he did not slacken the speed of his horses, and she wondered with a sudden fear what could have occurred.

Then she saw their arms waving, their glinting white teeth and heard them cheering.

The *Comte* drew his horses to a standstill.

'Welcome! Welcome!'

The words seemed to be repeated over and over again, then Frédéric, the spokesman for the slaves, came forward to say:

'We wish, Master, offer congratulations! We know you very happy!'

Melita looked at the *Comte* in astonishment, but it was impossible to say anything above the noise of the cheers.

One of the small children brought to the side of the chaise a large bouquet of flowers almost as big as herself.

Melita bent down to take it and as she did so saw in the crowd surging around the chaise the dark eyes of Léonore.

She looked at the old woman and understood

228

who it was who had known they were married and alerted everyone to cheer them on their return.

The *Comte* stepped from the chaise and walked round it to assist Melita to alight.

He drew her onto the steps of the sugar distillery, then raising his hand for silence he said:

'On behalf of *Madame la Comtesse* and myself, I thank you for your welcome.'

There was a burst of cheering at this and when he could make himself heard the *Comte* said:

'Tomorrow will be a feast day, there will be roast pig and everyone will enjoy their favourite dishes, and afterwards my wife and I will wish to see you dance and hear you sing.'

Again there was a wild burst of cheers. Then, having offered Melita his arm, the *Comte* drew her away from the crowd up the incline towards the house.

When they were out of ear-shot of the chattering and excited slaves Melita asked:

'How did they know? How could they be sure that we were married?'

'News in Martinique is carried on the wind,' the *Comte* smiled. 'There may be a dozen perfectly reasonable explanations, but I suspect that it was Léonore who was aware of it first.'

229

'That is what I thought,' Melita said simply.

They reached the house and now, as they stepped onto the verandah, Melita held her breath.

There was somone moving inside the Salon and she thought it must be *Madame* Boisset, until as they entered the room she saw it was a man.

He gave an exclamation of surprise when he saw them and walked towards the *Comte* with his hand outstretched.

'You have arrived too quickly for it to be possible that you received my message, *Monsieur le Comte.*'

'Doctor Dubocq!' the *Comte* exclaimed. 'Is anything wrong?'

'I am afraid there is,' the Doctor replied.

He looked at Melita before he said:

'Pardon, *Monsieur,* but I would prefer to speak with you alone.'

'That is unnecessary,' the *Comte* replied. 'Melita, let me introduce Doctor Dubocq, who is an old friend of the family, and has been our physician for some years. Doctor, this is my wife! We were married yesterday!'

The Doctor looked surprised but the smile on his face was warm.

'Your servant, *Madame,*' he said to Melita giving her an old-fashioned bow, 'and my heartfelt felicitations, *Monsieur le Comte*. May I wish you every possible happiness!'

'That is what we have just been wished by the slaves,' the *Comte* smiled.

'It is a pity you could not have returned to Vesonne under more cheerful circumstances,' the Doctor said slowly.

'What has happened?' the *Comte* asked.

'Rose-Marie!' Melita ejaculated in sudden fear.

'No, *Madame*. Rose-Marie is perfectly well and because I did not wish her to see *Madame* Boisset being taken from the house I suggested she went with a maid to visit the dumb boy who makes those dolls so cleverly.'

'You say that *Madame* Boisset has left the house?' she *Comte* asked quietly.

'That is what I have to tell you,' the Doctor replied. 'I was sent for early this morning by the maid, Eugénie, who informed me that *Madame* was ill.'

Melita held her breath.

'It appears she had taken some poison, obviously inadvertently, which made her extremely ill with pains and nausea. That was understandable, but it also affected her brain.'

The *Comte* was tense, but he did not speak.

'You were of course aware, *Monsieur*,' the Doctor continued, 'of the taint that existed in

231

Madame Boisset's immediate family?'

'What taint?' the *Comte* asked.

The Doctor looked surprised.

'I thought that *Monsieur* Calviare would have mentioned it to you.'

'He told me nothing.'

The Doctor pursed his lips for a moment, then he said:

'*Madame* Boisset's mother was, before she died, incurably mad!'

'I was never told that!' the *Comte* explained.

'The family was ashamed of it and tried to keep it secret. It was an inherited affliction: neither her mother nor her grandmother died in full possession of their senses.'

'I should have been informed of this,' the *Comte* said harshly.

'Most certainly you should have been,' the Doctor agreed, 'but although I have attended *Madame* Boisset only occasionally in the past years she always seemed to me to be quite level-headed and normal.'

'And when you came this morning?' the *Comte* questioned.

'Then it was very different,' the Doctor replied. 'Not only was she ill with the poison which Eugénie told me she might have taken in a glass of wine, but she was also mentally disturbed.'

The Doctor paused and Melita could see that something was troubling him. Then he said:

'I should be failing in my duty, *Monsieur,* if I did not tell you that while *Madame* was delirious she averred over and over again that she had been responsible for the death of your first wife.'

For a moment there was silence. Then the *Comte* said:

'What you have told me, Doctor, confirms some evidence that has been brought to my attention only in the last twenty-four hours.'

Again there was silence until the *Comte* said:

'I hope there is no reason for this to become public knowledge?'

'No, of course not,' the Doctor replied. 'I have taken *Madame* Boisset to the Hospital where she will have every possible care, but quite frankly there is no question as far as I can see of her ever again becoming normal, nor is it likely that she will live long.'

He paused before he said:

'I am not a brain specialist, but in my experience the tumours which affect the brain usually grow very quickly, and if *Madame* Boisset survives for more than a month or so I shall be surprised.'

'Thank you for being so frank,' the *Comte* said, 'and thank you for arranging that these developments should not affect my daughter, nor, I hope, my wife.'

He glanced at Melita as he spoke and she realised that he did not wish her to stay any longer while he discussed the details of the case with the Doctor.

She therefore laid for one moment her hand on his arm, expressing in that gesture her love, her understanding and her sympathy. Then she curtsied to the Doctor and left the Salon.

She ran up the stairs and along the passage to the School-Room.

As she half-expected, Eugénie was there sitting sewing at the table and she jumped to her feet when Melita appeared.

'You back, *M'mselle!*'

'I am back, the *Comte* is with me, and we are married, Eugénie!'

'Married?' Eugénie flung up her arms in an expression of elation and joy.

'That good news, *M'mselle*...I mean *Madame*. Very good news. Now the Master happy and everything well for us all.'

'Everything will be very well,' Melita answered.

She paused, then she said:

'I have to thank you, Eugénie. I realise that you saved my life.'

Eugénie nodded her head, but she did not

speak and Melita continued:

'You knew that *Madame* was responsible for the death of Rose-Marie's mother?'

Again Eugénie nodded.

Melita drew in her breath.

'The *Comte* and I cannot thank you enough for the love you have given Rose-Marie.'

'She my baby,' Eugénie said. 'If I tell about *Madame* she send me away. Best I stay and say nothing.'

'Yes, of coure. You were right,' Melita agreed. 'But now everything will be different and there will be no rows or angry words to frighten Rose-Marie.'

'That good, Mistress, very good.'

Melita smiled at the word 'Mistress'. Now she knew she was really accepted. Now she was part of the plantation with the *Comte* who was Master.

'Now you marry I move your clothes,' Eugénie was saying. 'Very pretty new gown, Mistress.'

'And there is a lovely wedding gown on the chaise,' Melita replied.

Automatically she moved along the passage towards her old room.

She opened the door.

It was just as she had left it, except for one thing—the doll which resembled Cécile

235

was no longer there.

She stared at the table on which it had stood.

Had she perhaps dreamt it? Had it just been an illusion?

She wanted to ask Eugénie where it had gone, then felt it was better if she said nothing. Let the past take care of the past. All that mattered was the future.

She walked to the window to look out over the plantation towards the sea.

It was the window where she had heard the beat of the drum which had called her into the forest.

There was, however, no time for introspection, for she heard Rose-Marie's voice calling for her and her footsteps come running up the stairs.

'*Mademoiselle! Mademoiselle!* You are back!'

The child burst into the room and flung her arms round her neck.

'You are back, and I missed you! Papa has come home too. I am so glad. So very, very glad!'

'And I am glad to be back, darling,' Melita said truthfully.

She knelt down on the floor so that she was level with Rose-Marie's face and said softly:

'I have something to tell you.'

'I know what it is,' Rose-Marie said. 'Léonore told me. You are married to Papa and now you are my Mama!'

'Yes, I am,' Melita said, apprehensive in case Rose-Marie should resent her taking her mother's place.

The child's arms went round her neck again as she said:

'Now I have a Papa and a Mama like other children, and you will never go away, will you?'

'Never for good,' Melita promised. 'Sometimes your Papa and I must have a little holiday together, but we will always come home.'

Rose-Marie hugged her frantically and Melita felt the tears prick her eyes so she said quickly:

'If you run downstairs to the chaise which by now must be at the front door I think you will find there is a special parcel for you. It is quite a big one, and it is underneath the seat on which your Papa and I were sitting.'

Rose-Marie gave a cry of delight and sped down the stairs while Melita took off her bonnet and smoothed her hair. For the moment she felt shy of moving into the other room to which Eugénie was already carrying her clothes.

She had never seen where the *Comte* slept but she knew it was what Eugénie and the maids called "The Master's Room".

She was aware that it consisted of two bedchambers and a Sitting-Room with windows overlooking the garden at the back and the orchards sloping down to the forest where the *Comte* had kissed her.

Melita could not bear to think about *Madame* Boisset and what would happen to her; her mind shied away from dwelling on the horror of it.

At the same time she was thankful with a feeling of inexpressible relief that there would be no recriminations as she had expected there would be on their return to Vesonne.

Now the *Comte* would not even have to explain that the will *Madame* Boisset forced Cécile to write was no longer valid, nor would he be obliged to accuse her of having caused her death.

It was as if the sunshine had swept away all the shadows and now there was not a cloud in the sky.

It was not surprising that the slaves had cheered from sheer happiness because the *Comte* was once again in control and their Master, as he had been before.

Melita walked slowly down the stairs.

She did not intend to go into the Salon where she thought the *Comte* and the Doctor might still be talking, but into a smaller room next door to it, and from there onto the verandah to find Rose-Marie.

But the door of the Salon was open and the Doctor had gone. Rose-Marie, alone with the *Comte,* was drawing from the box the huge doll with eyes that opened and shut which they had bought for her in St. Pierre.

'She is pretty, Papa!' Rose-Marie was saying, 'the prettiest doll I have ever seen! But I still love Philippe's even though they do not last for long.'

'I think Philippe made you a doll this morning, did he not?' Melita asked, stepping into the Salon.

She saw the *Comte's* eyes light up at the sight of her and she smiled at him as she waited for his daughter's reply.

'Yes,' Rose-Marie answered. 'He gave me a doll that he had nearly ready for me when I went to see him. He said it was to be a surprise for me and for you. Shall I fetch it to show you?'

'Yes, of course, dearest,' Melita said.

'I left it on the verandah when I came back to the house,' Rose-Marie explained. 'I was frightened of dropping it as I ran up the stairs.'

She went from the Salon onto the verandah and the *Comte* held out his arms to Melita.

She moved towards him feeling secure and safe in a manner that she had never felt before.

Now she had come like a ship into harbour and the sea was no longer rough, nor was there any threat of a storm.

He held her close as if he understood what she was feeling. Then Rose-Marie came back with her doll.

'Look, Papa,' she said, 'Philippe has made me a bride!'

The doll was exquisite, all in white leaves which came from a special shrub which Melita had seen in the garden. The face was white, too, and the hair was golden.

Melita's fingers tightened on the *Comte's*.

They said nothing in front of Rose-Marie, and there were so many things to do during the day and so many things to see to that it was not until the evening after dinner that they had a chance to talk quietly together.

It was then that the *Comte* drew Melita across the lawn and she knew he was taking her to the *Pomme d'Amour* where he had first told her of his love.

She was wearing her white wedding gown and in the light from the moon which was rising in the sky above them she looked ethereal, and yet somehow intrinsically a part of the flowers and the fragrance of the night.

Without speaking they moved downhill over the soft grass until they reached the tree where he had found her looking up into the blossom.

'So much has happened since we were here,' Melita said, speaking for the first time since they had left the house.

'My dreams have come true,' the *Comte* said. 'You are my wife, Vesonne is mine again, and we seem to be enveloped, my darling, in an aura of happiness.'

'That is what I feel too,' Melita said looking up at him.

It was possible in the moonlight for them to see each other's faces and the *Comte* thought the stars were reflected in Melita's eyes.

'I am so grateful, I am afraid to question anything that has happened, and yet so much remains unanswered,' she said. 'So many things are strange and mysterious, and for which there appears to be no explanation.'

'Does it matter?' the *Comte* asked. 'We are together. You are mine and I love you beyond words!'

Melita gave a deep sigh, then she said:

'It is all wonderful, quite perfect, and yet perhaps I am a little...afraid.'

Once again he knew what she was thinking.

'Of Voodoo?' he asked. 'Forget it, my precious. If, as the Negros believe, they can bring back the spirits of the dead, then the spirits they bring are those we deserve.'

241

He knew that Melita was listening intently and he went on:

'A good person will evoke good spirits and a bad person evil. Therefore Voodoo need never concern you, my darling, because you are good and there is no evil of any sort in your mind or soul.'

'It is...still...magic,' Melita murmured.

He laughed softly and turned her face up to his.

'The only magic with which we need concern ourselves,' he said, 'is the magic of love, the magic you have brought me, and because of it I am bound to you by a spell that has captured me and made me your prisoner from now to eternity.'

Melita would have answered him, but his lips came down on hers and it was impossible to think of anything but the wonder of his touch and the thrill which ran through her like a fire.

She knew that she excited him and felt an excitement to equal his, rising within her.

He drew her closer and still closer and now it seemed to Melita as if the whole world and the Heavens themselves disappeared.

There was no forest, no stars, no moon. There was only the wild, ecstatic rapture of the *Comte's* lips, the beat of their hearts and the need of their bodies and their minds

242

for each other.

This was love.

This was the magic beyond all other magic—
the love that casts out evil.